JOHN RUSSELL FEARN

ROBBERY WITHOUT VIOLENCE

Complete and Unabridged

LINFORD
Leicester

Gloucestershire County Council Library	

British Library CIP Data

Fearn, John Russell, *1908 – 1960*
    Robbery without violence.—Large print ed.—
Linford mystery library
    1. Robbery investigation—Fiction
    2. Detective and mystery stories
    3. Large type books
    I. Title
    823.9′12 [F]

    ISBN 1–84617–373–6

Published by
F. A. Thorpe (Publishing)
Anstey, Leicestershire

Set by Words & Graphics Ltd.
Anstey, Leicestershire
Printed and bound in Great Britain by
T. J. International Ltd., Padstow, Cornwall

This book is printed on acid-free paper

ROBBERY WITHOUT VIOLENCE

When fifty million pounds worth of gold vanishes overnight from an impregnable bank vault, Chief Inspector Hargraves of Scotland Yard finds himself completely baffled. And when the owner of the bank dies in mysterious circumstances, Hargraves is again spurred to seek outside help from scientist Sawley Garson, a specialist in solving 'impossible' crimes. But can even he explain the inexplicable?

1

Mackinley's bank, just off London's Throgmorton Street, was busy. And not only busy, but extremely nervous.

The newspapers had made a feast of the fact that on this day, Tuesday, Mackinley's were to receive a massive consignment of gold. No less than £50,000,000 worth of yellow metal in one consignment, practically the entire wealth of a certain small foreign state, transferred to Britain for safe keeping.

In itself the amount was not really astronomical, but to receive it all in one lump was certainly something of a phenomenon. It produced headaches in all directions.

Police by the score were on duty outside the bank: steel-plated wagons kept watch from strategic positions; while in the bank itself, plainclothesmen mingled with Scotland Yard officials as the precious ingots were removed from the armor-plated trucks which had been driven straight from the airport.

Gold!

Fifty million pounds worth of it, and every criminal in Britain and elsewhere knew it was being taken into the bank.

The responsibility was enormous, particularly for Joseph Mackinley, the managing director of the bank, who ceaselessly watched the proceedings from a window of his private office.

'I'll be glad when this business is over!'

He had said this for about the 20th time, pausing in between to mop his face.

And each time his head cashier, Clive Burton, had merely murmured an assent. Like his employer, he felt, too, as though he were temporarily living on an unexploded bomb that would go off at any moment.

At intervals Mackinley deserted his office and his big, heavy figure was visible among the employees, inquiring into the progress of depositing the gold in the strong vault.

He got the same answer each time — everything was in order. And at last, toward 4 in the afternoon, the job was done.

Mackinley stood with the head cashier and fellow-directors watching as the foot-thick steel door was closed on the strong vault, and the first locks clicked into place.

'That's better,' Mackinley said, with a sigh of relief. 'Most decidedly better.' He sharpened up and looked at Burton.

'You fully understand the regulations governing this particular lot of gold, Mr. Burton?'

'Fully, sir.' Burton was an urbane, small-built man, with rimless eyeglasses, 'This main strong vault is not to contain anything else but the gold until I receive other instructions. The door is to be time-locked, and each morning I am to inspect the gold, for routine purposes, then again time-lock the door for 24 hours.'

'That is correct . . . ' For the first time Mackinley relaxed and smiled. 'Well, gentlemen, that completes the business, I think. Thank you for your co-operation.'

With that he went back to his private

office, and the banking staff did not see him for the rest of the working day.

Not that this was unusual. Mackinley was not often on view. He existed in a region of opulent furniture and soft carpets, owner and controller of the wealthy bank he had created, but content in the main to leave its operations to the care of a trusted staff.

Mackinley's Bank was a household word.

That evening, when he arrived back at his luxurious London home, Mackinley felt and looked a contented man. His ruddy face was pink; his blue eyes bright, and his immaculate gray hair impeccably brushed.

And at the same moment that Mackinley arrived home, his daughter Judith was stepping from a silver-plated limousine in the center of London, outside Debney's high-class restaurant.

She smiled at her chauffeur as he held the door for her.

'That will be all, Lomax,' she said briefly. 'I shan't need you again.'

'Yes, miss.'

Lomax carefully closed the rear door and returned to the front seat of the vehicle. The limousine glided away silently into the traffic.

Judith crossed the pavement and entered the restaurant, stepping into the soft lights and gentle music of Debney's.

The headwaiter, ever-vigilant, immediately recognized the wealthy young woman in the mink coat, and hastened across to her.

'Good evening, Miss Mackinley.'

'Hello, Alberti.' She looked at him with frank brown eyes, a girl entirely unspoiled by money, and yet revelling in it just the same. 'Mr. Cole here yet?'

'I have not seen him, Miss Mackinley, even though I have kept careful watch,' the headwaiter said apologetically. He smiled. 'But no doubt he will be here shortly . . . The usual table, I assume?'

'Yes. The usual table.'

Judith followed Alberti across the room, and in another moment she was seated at the quiet table that she invariably had.

She slipped the fur coat from her wide

shoulders and handed it to Alberti for safekeeping.

Seconds later another waiter appeared with a carafe of water and two glasses. As the girl nodded he poured out one glass and retired.

Judith sipped at her water and prepared to wait. Her wait was not a long one, for presently a young man appeared, handsome after a fashion, in a well-cut lounge suit.

He slipped into the seat opposite and smiled an apology.

'Sorry, Judy — something kept me at the last minute.'

'I imagined it must be that.' Judith's hand touched his for a moment, then they relaxed as the headwaiter, who had been discretely watching from a distance, glided towards their table.

The young man glanced up.

'The usual, Alberti,' he said.

Alberti vanished soundlessly and Jefferson Cole gave an audible sigh, almost of relief it seemed.

Judith frowned slightly.

'Anything the matter?' she asked briefly.

Cole smiled apologetically and gave a little shrug.

'Of course not, dear. Absolutely nothing except the delay in getting here — and then one thing after another kept popping up at the garage. Anyway I didn't forget the table. I booked it first thing this morning. I knew you'd understand if I happened to be late.'

'Of course. I know how hard you are working these days.'

For a moment there was silence. Jeff Cole looked before him absently.

'Things all right at the garage?' Judith asked him suddenly.

'All right?' he queried vaguely.

'Last time we met you told me you were not sure how things were going, whether you were going to extend the business or not.'

'Oh, that!' Cole relaxed and smiled faintly. 'Yes, everything's fine. I'll definitely be making the extensions I mentioned. You realize what that means, of course?'

Judith smiled. 'Why do you think I asked you? You don't suppose I enjoy waiting to be married, do you? I want to get on with it — get our lives planned. Matter of fact, I can't fathom why you've delayed so long.'

'I told you — just so that I could be sure of my ground.'

'But how absurd! Sure of your ground with a garage prospering like yours?'

Jeff hesitated a fraction, then smiled. 'Perhaps I'm over-cautious,' he admitted. 'Or rather — I have been over-cautious. It's all ended now. I know exactly what I aim to do.'

He fell silent again as Alberti returned with their first course; then as the meal progressed he asked:

'Is your father any more amenable towards me than he was?'

'Matter of fact I'm afraid he isn't. He still thinks I oughtn't to marry anything less than a prince. He shudders at the very thought of a garage owner. But I'll talk him around, never fear.'

'In my estimation,' Jeff said, 'a garage owner is every bit as important to the community as a banker. Besides your dad is in the 60s and I'm only in the 30s. By the time I'm his age I'll gamble I've as much power and notoriety as he has.'

'Banking and your sort of trade are a bit different,' Judith smiled

'Maybe, but I have other — ' Jeff stopped suddenly, seemed to think of something then abruptly changed the subject. 'Anyway we'll see. With you at my side I'll conquer the earth, if need be. The only thing worrying me is that your father may put a stop to things.'

'How exactly?'

'I don't know — but he's a man with a good deal of influence and the devil of a lot of money. With those two weapons he can do a good deal toward spoiling our fun if he feels like it.'

'Let him try!' Judith's lips tightened for a moment. 'I'm legal age and he can't tell me what to do. The most he can do is cut me out of his will, and that won't worry me as long as I have you.'

Jeff's hands stole across the table again and seized the girl's tightly.

'Thanks, Judy. I know your dad's chief objection to me is that I haven't enough money — in his view — to be worth the attention of his daughter. Before very long I think he'll have to change his tune very forcibly. What with the extension to the garage, and other things — '

Judith contented herself with a smile because she did not think it necessary to say anything. In her own mind she was quite decided.

There would never be any other man for her but Jefferson Cole.

2

Clive Burton, head cashier of the Mackinley Bank, passed a particularly restless night after the events of the day. In consequence he arrived at the bank the following morning in an anything but cheerful mood and his usual urbanity down at zero.

As he walked across the wealth of marble-tiled floor toward his office, morosely surveying the empty counters and the bare spaces behind the grilles as he went, he caught sight of the night watchman emerging from his quarters at the farther end of the wilderness.

'Everything all right, Anderson?' he called sharply.

Anderson was due to leave when the first of the day staff arrived, and he had never been known to be late for this appointment. He came shuffling across the tiles, scarf tied about his neck and old trilby pulled down over his eyes.

Immense integrity and the ability to keep awake at night had earned Anderson his post, and nobody had had any reason to complain of his nocturnal vigilance.

'Yes, Mr. Burton, everything's all right. Nothing's happened all night.'

'I'm glad to hear it,' Burton retorted shortly. 'Somehow I had rather expected trouble.'

'Trouble?' Anderson looked puzzled. 'Why's that?'

'Hang it, man, don't you read the papers?' Burton exclaimed. 'Don't you know that 50 million in gold was lodged in this bank yesterday?'

Anderson scratched the back of his neck.

'Aye, now you come to mention it, I did read something about it — but then things are so watertight these days there ain't nothing to fear . . . Well, I'll be on my way, Mr. Burton. Got to get my kip, you know. Good-day to you.'

★　★　★

Burton walked the length of the tiled hall and vanished in the brick-walled region beyond. He finally went down into the basement, switched on all the lights, and finished his trip in front of the giant, impregnable door of the main strong-room.

He waited a moment or two; glanced at the electric clock, then smiled as there came a distinct click from the strongroom door. The time switch had operated dead to the second.

In a matter of moments, Burton had the enormous door open. It moved easily on its perfectly balanced hinges.

Again switching on the lights, he moved into the interior of the strongroom and surveyed the steel-walled section where the gold had been stacked the previous day —

Had been stacked?

Burton dragged to a standstill, staring. His common sense said one thing and his brain and eyes said another.

There was no gold! Not a brick, not an ingot, a trace! The steel-walled corner specially used for such deposits was empty.

By very slow degrees Burton found the power of movement. He turned and began to run, yelling for members of the staff in general, and for Joseph Mackinley in particular.

A teller arrived first — the chief teller — and he nearly collided with Burton as he came dashing up the basement steps.

'What's the matter, Mr. Burton?' he asked in surprise. 'Something happened?'

'The — the gold in the vault,' Burton gulped, his eyes staring. 'It's not there!'

'Not there! But that's impossible!'

'I know it's impossible, you fool, but it's happened! At least I think it has.'

'Think it has!' the teller exclaimed, glancing back at the others crowding down the basement steps.

'Maybe my eyes are wrong, or something.' Burton was looking sick. 'Go and look, Edwards. Go and look!'

Burton swayed. He might even have fallen if the assortment of tellers and cashiers around him hadn't supported him. Edwards went leaping down the stairs and a ghastly silence followed.

Then he came back slowly into view.

'Yes,' Edwards said, staring up. 'It's gone! The whole lot of it! It was ceiling-high when it was put in.'

'Where's Mr. Mackinley?' Burton asked abruptly.

'Not here yet, sir. It's only a little after 9.'

'Yes. Yes — of course.'

Burton shook himself and tried to get a grip on things. Slowly he went up the remainder of the stairs and then stood in the tiled hall, thinking.

The staff came up behind him, waiting.

'I suppose,' Burton said at last, 'that I should send for the police immediately — but I'd better wait and see what Mr. Mackinley says. In the meantime I'll check if the closed-circuit tv cameras picked anything up.'

'Yes, sir.'

'As you say, Mr. Burton.'

Everybody was extraordinarily polite, and nobody knew what to make of the situation. Gradually the staff disbanded and moved to their different working positions in readiness for the day's business.

As for Burton, he was almost deaf, dumb and blind to everything — as well he might be. The gold had been entrusted to him.

Outside Mackinley, he was the only one who knew the combination of the time lock. Whichever way he looked at it, the situation was alarming.

Pulling himself together, Burton let himself into the room containing the closed-circuit television monitor screen. Half afraid of what he might see, he fast-forwarded through the recordings from the previous night and early morning.

As he watched, his bafflement and sense of foreboding increased. Apart from the night watchman himself, they appeared to clearly show that absolutely nobody else had entered the bank.

If anything, this increased Burton's nervousness. If nobody had entered the bank during the night, then how had the gold been stolen?

But even with fifty million in gold missing, business carries on — on the surface — as usual. It did so at

Mackinley's Bank, and Mackinley himself certainly saw nothing unusual when eventually he arrived toward 10.30.

Within five minutes, however, the blow had fallen.

Mackinley had barely settled himself at his desk, about to select his first cigar of the day, when there came a heavy knock on his door.

Before he could answer, the door burst open, and Burton came into the room.

Mackinley lost the expression of pleasant benevolence, but checked the angry expostulation on his lips as he caught sight of Burton's strained features.

The chief cashier sank down, uninvited, into a seat near the desk. He leaned forward, gulped nervously, and said:

'The gold's gone! Every bit of it — '

Mackinley's heavy features registered a range of emotions as he listened to Burton's halting account of the events. Anger gave way to sheer disbelief.

'But — but it's fantastic!' he declared flatly, as a genuinely frightened Burton finished telling him of the facts. 'Absolutely fantastic! It couldn't happen!'

'But it did, sir. And as I've said, I didn't rely on my own judgment. I had others look as well. There's no doubt about it. The gold has gone.'

Mackinley finally lighted his cigar and then looked at the glowing end broodingly. The disbelief on his face had changed to grim worry.

'Have you told Scotland Yard?' he asked briefly.

'I haven't told anybody but you, sir. I wanted your suggestions.'

'Get Scotland Yard immediately! In any case, the staff knows about it, and with all respect to their vows of secrecy, one of them will let the cat out of the bag. We've got to get action. Once this news hits the papers I'll be ruined!'

'Surely not, sir — '

Mackinley banged his fist on the desk. 'Look here, Burton, would you trust a bank that lets fifty million in gold slide out of its strong vault? I wouldn't, and that's flat!'

As Burton dithered, the magnate added: 'Never mind, I'll get the Yard myself.'

Mackinley whipped up the telephone; then glanced again at the distraught Burton.

'Pull yourself together man, and get back on the job. And not a word more about this: it's up to the police to handle it. At all costs we must try to keep it out of the papers — Hello, that Scotland Yard? This is Joseph Mackinley speaking — '

And so Mackinley set the wheels turning. Within 15 minutes Chief Inspector Hargraves was on the spot, accompanied by Detective Sergeant Harry Brice and a couple of ordinary constables. They arrived unobtrusively and were admitted to the bank by a rear door.

They were met by Mackinley and Burton, and as Mackinley nodded to him the head cashier again related the facts.

The main points had already been given by the magnate in his telephone call, but Hargraves listened without interruption until Burton had finished his personal account.

'And you say you've examined the

bank's closed-circuit television recordings — which showed nothing?' Hargraves asked sharply, looking at the hapless Burton.

'Well, just briefly, Chief Inspector. I've only fast-forwarded through them: there hasn't really been time . . . '

Hargraves turned to one of his constables. 'Better take a closer look, Harkins.' He looked back enquiringly at Burton. 'Can you fix that?'

Burton glanced at Mackinley, who nodded his assent. As Burton and the constable left the group, Hargraves turned back to the magnate.

'Now I'd like to see the strongroom for myself, Mr. Mackinley,' he said, and the other nodded grimly.

'Of course. Follow me, gentlemen.'

He led the way down the basement steps, and thence to the basement itself and the still open strongroom.

Sergeant Brice made a swift examination of the door lock, being careful not to touch it. Then he looked back at his superior. 'Absolutely no sign of forced entry sir.'

'Naturally,' the chief inspector said, as Mackinley stood beside him, 'I remember the gold being placed here since I had a detail of men on guard duty during the process. And now the gold has obviously gone. Right!'

Mackinley did not say anything. He felt too sick with worry.

Hargraves frowned as a thought struck him. He dropped to one knee and examined the floor. It appeared to be solid metal.

'Could someone have dug a tunnel underneath here and taken out the gold that way?' His tone betrayed the fact that he did not really think this was a possibility.

Mackinley shook his head impatiently. 'Not a chance. The foundations are solid concrete and you can see for yourself that the metal floor is completely intact.'

Feeling slightly foolish, Hargraves straightened up and tried another tack.

'You say there was a watchman on duty all night?' he questioned. 'Where can I get hold of him?'

Mackinley made a bothered movement.

'It will be in the files. I'll see you have his address and phone number.'

'Very good.' Hargraves considered a while, a tall, lean-faced man, not easily moved. 'And you yourself, Mr. Mackinley. Where were you last evening?'

'Where was I?' the magnate frowned. 'Does that matter?'

'With deference, sir, yes. It matters where everybody was, but you in particular, and Mr. Burton. You are the only ones who know the combination of the safe time lock.'

Mackinley seemed about to protest at what he took to be a slur on his character, then he relaxed.

'Hmmm, I see what you mean,' he admitted. 'I can't answer for Mr. Burton, of course, but I was at home all evening — and I can prove it.'

The inspector's eyes strayed to Burton, who had just rejoined the group, leaving P.C. Harkins to study the CCTV tapes.

'Can you account for your movements last night, Mr. Burton?'

'I can, yes. I went to a political meeting at the city hall.'

'Can anyone vouch for that?' Hargraves questioned.

'Yes. I met several friends while I was there, so they'll be able to verify the point.'

'Quite so.' Hargraves gave a disarming smile. 'Don't misunderstand me, gentlemen. I have to treat everybody alike in this matter. And I don't think you have yet realized how extraordinarily difficult this business is.'

Mackinley said abruptly: 'It's the utter impossibility of this business that gets me down! How could all that gold be taken from this vault? How could it? And without anyone being seen or heard?'

'On the face of it, it just couldn't happen,' the chief inspector replied. 'But it did! And as long as there is a reason it's our job to find it. I've already sent for fingerprint men and photographers. Once we have something to go on we'll swing into action. Meanwhile, I shall not need to trouble you gentlemen further for the moment.'

Mackinley took the dismissal with good grace and returned to his office with

Burton trailing silently behind him.

Hargraves detailed the remaining constable to join his colleague checking the closed-circuit tv recordings. 'And report back to headquarters as soon as you can, and bring the recordings with you, as evidence.'

He lit a cigarette and dragged on it thoughtfully.

'Evidence?' Sergeant Brice asked dryly. 'Of what, sir? Any ideas?'

'If my name were Merlin I might have. As it is, I'm completely stumped . . . '

Now entirely alone in the strong vault, the two men continued to stare unbelievingly at its blank, metal-lined expanse. Then Sergeant Brice spoke again.

'I've come up against a few things in my time, sir, but none of them was like this. There isn't the vaguest hint of a clue, and usually there's at least *something*.'

He was on the point of speaking again when the fingerprint men and photographer arrived. They came into the strongroom with something of an air of wonder.

'Morning, boys.' Hargraves gave a brief

nod. 'And what's the matter with you? Never seen the inside of a strongroom before?'

'It's not that,' the photographer said, setting up his reflex. 'We've heard the story of the vanishing gold and we're just beginning to wonder if somebody didn't dream the whole thing.'

'Nobody dreamed anything,' Hargraves said grimly. 'It's all hard, relentless fact. And I've more than a sneaking suspicion that we're going to be up against it. However — do your stuff.'

For a long time there was silence as powder and insufflator came into operation. Hargraves stood in deep thought during the process, juggling the problem in his mind.

When eventually the fingerprint man had finished Hargraves looked at him questioningly.

'Well? Any joy?'

'Plenty of fingerprints, chief inspector, but from the look of 'em I'd say they're the sort of prints you'd expect to find from members of the staff. They're in the same place — a complete jumble of them

— and there isn't a clear impression in the lot of 'em.'

'Nothing on the walls?'

'Not a thing.'

'Where are these prints you mention?'

'Around the door edges and on the lock, the sort of prints you would inevitably get by unlocking the door and then grabbing hold of it.'

'Mmmm — which doesn't tell us much. Even if there were clear prints, the law doesn't entitle me to check the bank staff's prints for comparison.'

Hargraves looked at the photographer. 'Got your stuff, Terry?'

'Usual views,' Terry replied phlegmatically. 'A strongroom has no glamour angles anyhow.'

'Okay. Leave the prints in my office when they're done.'

The photographer and fingerprint man both nodded and then went on their way. Hargraves sighed and scratched the back of his neck.

'Frankly, sir,' Sergeant Brice said, 'I just don't know where to start. Usually there's always something — '

'So you said before,' Hargraves remarked testily. 'Well, there's nothing more we can do here,' he decided. 'We'd best get back to the office and decide our plan of campaign from there.'

As they went up the basement steps, Hargraves added:

'You had better pick up that night watchman's address from Mackinley, and at the same time have somebody check on Burton's alibi.'

3

At 3 o'clock that same afternoon Henry Anderson, the night watchman at Mackinley's Bank, found himself closeted with Chief Inspector Hargraves and the inevitable Sergeant Brice.

Anderson was not looking immensely co-operative, either. He had been awakened from sleep in order to keep the appointment.

'This won't keep you long, Mr. Anderson,' Hargraves apologized, smiling. 'It has to be done, though. I presume the sergeant has told you what has happened at the bank?'

'Yes, I know.' Anderson moistened his lips and peered from his myopic gray eyes. 'But you're wasting your time picking on me. I did no thievin'. I'm an honest man.'

'Nobody doubts that for a moment, Mr. Anderson — but you fill a rather significant role in that you were the only person on hand at the approximate time the gold was stolen.'

'You know the time, then?'

'I'm afraid not, but we know it happened during the night when you were on duty.'

'How can you be sure of that?' The old man's jaw began to project argumentatively.

'Because it's obvious,' Hargraves replied, quite controlled.

'I say it isn't. That gold, so I'm told, was put in the strongroom toward 4 in the afternoon. It was found to have gone when Mr. Burton opened up this morning. I don't come on duty till 7. There's three hours when something could have happened — three hours in which I was not there. Why pick on me?'

Hargraves cleared his throat. 'I agree that there were three hours in which something could have occurred, but I am quite satisfied that nothing did. The time when that gold was stolen was obviously when vigilance was at its slackest — during the night, when the normal bank staff were absent. Didn't you, Mr.

Anderson, hear anything during that time?'

'Not a thing.'

'How far were you from the strong-room?'

'Quite a little distance. The strongroom is in the basement, as you know, and my small office where I have my chow and a sit-down is on the ground floor. Naturally, I always keep my office door open when I'm in there, and from it I have a clear view of the basement steps.'

'And nobody went down them?'

'No — or came up, either. I can swear to that. As I keep on telling you: there wasn't a sound all night.'

'What,' Hargraves asked, 'is your office like?'

'Ain't much. There's a chair and a table, on which are a telephone and a set of alarm buttons in case anything happens — which last night it didn't. Oh, and a small radio. I spend a lot of time listening to it — turned down low, of course. I asked Mr. Mackinley if I could,' he added, as Hargraves raised an eyebrow in mild reproof.

'Would it be loud enough to drown any slight sounds somewhere in the building?'

Anderson thought for a moment, then he sighed. 'Come to that, I suppose it would. But I'd hear anything loud,' he went on earnestly. 'And I maintain that nobody could've removed that much gold without making a sound of some kind.'

'Quite true, but the fact that your attention was distracted by the radio is interesting because — '

'Wait a minute!' Anderson exclaimed suddenly, a faraway look in his eyes. 'I've just thought of something. I didn't have the radio on last night after 10 o'clock because of interference. It was so bad it drowned the program.'

Hargraves frowned slightly. 'Drowned the program? Around 10 o'clock? What program was it?'

'Singing festival from the Albert Hall. National program on the BBC.'

'Hmmm. I listened to that for a time as well, but I didn't notice any interference. Could have been a local trouble, of course.'

'Whatever it was it finished things for

me. I had to switch the radio off.'

Hargraves nodded rather tiredly. 'All right, Mr. Anderson. Thanks for coming along. Just routine, you understand.'

Anderson grunted something, picked up his battered hat, and then departed.

Hargraves sat in silence, lost in moody speculations.

'Not much gravy in that, sir,' Brice remarked, glancing up from the typewritten notes he had made of the brief interview.

'No. That's the trouble.' Hargraves tapped the desk indecisively, his lips compressed. Then he went on:

'It's the absolute lack of anything to go on that has me stopped. PC Harkins has double-checked the bank's closed-circuit tv camera recordings, and agrees with what Burton told us earlier: nobody entered the bank during the night! And there's just nothing in Anderson's statement to give us a lead either.'

'Do you suspect him, sir?'

Hargraves waved a hand impatiently.

'As for suspecting Anderson — I'd as soon suspect my own grandfather! He's neither the wit, nor the strength, to contrive a major theft like this.'

Brice nodded and stood reflecting. Hargraves glanced at him.

'What about the alibis of Burton and Mackinley? Did you have them checked?'

'I did. Watertight in both cases. So now we're reduced to suspecting somebody in the general bank staff.'

Hargraves shook his head. 'I think they're clean enough. Let's look at the thing logically. That gold couldn't be removed without somebody opening the strongroom door. Right?'

'Right!'

'Only two men knew the combination of the time lock — Mackinley himself, and Burton. The rest of the staff didn't even know the combination.'

'Which indicates an outsider,' Brice said decisively.

'So I begin to think. There's no mystery as to how an outsider knew about the gold since the papers have been splashing the business for some time. An outsider, given the information as to when the gold would be put in the vault, only needed to work out how to get the gold out of the vault. That bit stumps us, but if we can get a lead on who attempted the feat we can at least start.'

'Anybody particular in mind?'

'No. It's difficult to pin down since gold would attract almost anybody. Might have a check-up made on all the big crooks we know and see what their movements were last night. Also have all people within range of the bank questioned. To get the gold out, there must have been activity of some kind, and it's possible that somebody saw something. A belated homecomer, an uneasy sleeper looking through the window, even a drunk maybe. Anyway, get all the information you can root out.'

'Right, sir. I'll do that. And you? Taking any special line?'

'I might have another word or two with Mackinley. A new angle occurs to me — This might conceivably be a crime with a double purpose. Revenge, as well as the material gain.'

'I'm not with you, sir,' Brice confessed.

'Mackinley may have a bitter and

ingenious enemy somewhere. It wouldn't be surprising for a man in his position. I might do worse than find out if there is such a person. If that person has the qualifications for pulling a trick like this I'll go further. Anyhow, it's worth a try. You follow your line and I'll follow mine. We'll check here later. Right?'

'Right!'

★ ★ ★

Joseph Mackinley was looking not at all happy when Hargraves was shown into his luxurious private office toward the close of the afternoon.

'Hello, Chief Inspector.' He rose from his desk and crossed over to shake hands, 'Any good news to bring me?'

'Afraid not, sir. I just came along to ask one or two further questions. Purely routine.'

'Questions?' Mackinley motioned to an armchair and then pushed over the cigar box as Hargraves seated himself.

Hargraves shook his head. 'Thanks, but no. Now, I have to ask you if — '

'Don't you fellows at the Yard do anything else beside ask questions?' Mackinley growled. 'This vanishing gold business is urgent — desperately so.'

'Quite so,' Hargraves said quietly. 'I assure you I am doing my best endeavours, but I can also understand your anxiety. The fact remains you'll have to trust the police because you can't do anything without them . . . Now, to a few questions. Have you any particular enemies?'

'I have a few — naturally.' Mackinley paced around the office with hands in trousers pockets.

'I'd like their names and addresses,' Hargraves said. 'Have no fear but that everything will be treated confidentially.'

Mackinley went to the desk, scribbled on a memo pad, and then handed it over.

'There they are, and not the least bit of use to you, I'm afraid.'

Hargraves glanced down the list. Quite a few of the names were those of men famous in Throgmorton Street and on the stock exchange. He smiled to himself and then asked another question:

'Anybody else, privately, who thoroughly dislikes you?'

'Privately?'

'As apart from your business life, I mean. This is not an attempt to pry into your domestic affairs, but it's possible there is something — or somebody.'

Mackinley shrugged. 'Nothing specific, I'm afraid. I've a wife who doesn't think I pay enough attention to her; a daughter who makes full use of the fact that I'm her wealthy father — and finally there's young Jeff Cole.'

'Cole?'

'Judy's so-called fiancé. Come to think of it, he doesn't like me a bit, but that's only because I strongly disapprove of his association with Judith.'

'Could I ask you to be more explicit,' Hargraves urged, making shorthand notes on the list of addresses Mackinley had given him.

'Explicit? In what way?'

'Your daughter and this Mr. Cole. Why do you disapprove of him?'

The Mackinley jaw set doggedly. 'He isn't high enough in the world for her.

Not enough influence or background. Think of it! The daughter of Joseph Mackinley married to a garage proprietor. It isn't to be thought of.'

'I'd rather like to see this Jeff Cole,' Hargraves said thoughtfully. 'What's his address?'

'He runs the Apex Garage on Morton Street — not far from here. He's there pretty well all day so you'll find him easily enough. But remember — this bank robbery is a secret! Nobody must know.'

'Sooner or later somebody's got to,' Hargraves answered bluntly. 'I'll be as discreet as possible. But first I'd like a few words with your daughter. When's a good time to catch her?'

'She ought to be at home now — And don't go telling her more than you have to. I'll do that myself.'

Hargraves rose to his feet. 'Your family is bound to know in the end, Mr. Mackinley, but I'll be as careful as I can. I'll have a chat with her and let you know when anything develops.'

Mackinley hesitated over adding some-thing, but he did not say it.

Hargraves left the office and went on his way, making his first call the Mackinley mansion.

A maidservant answered the door to him, and showed some astonishment as Hargraves showed his warrant card.

'I'm Chief Inspector Hargraves. Is Miss Judith Mackinley at home? I need to speak to her — urgently.'

The maid confirmed that Judith was at home, just as Mackinley had intimated she would be. She invited him into the house and ushered him into an enormous lounge.

He was asked to wait whilst the maid informed Mackinley's daughter of his visit.

Moments later, with an air of considerable surprise, Judith herself came sweeping prettily into the enormous lounge.

'You — you want me, Chief Inspector?' She seemed quite unable to credit the fact, even when Hargraves again displayed his warrant card.

'I think perhaps you can help me, Miss Mackinley.'

Hargraves motioned her to a chair.

'Help you?' Judith sat down slowly. 'But — but what have I done? Is it some parking offence that you've come about? Something I have done with the car, and shouldn't have?'

'Nothing like that,' Hargraves smiled. He sat down himself and then looked at the girl steadily. He decided he liked what he saw.

'This concerns a matter connected with your father's bank, Miss Mackinley. You don't know about it yet, but it is inevitable that you must.'

The brown eyes opened wide. 'The bank? But I don't know anything about the bank, except that father owns it.'

'Quite so. To cut the preamble, Miss Mackinley, fifty million in gold has been stolen from the bank and it's my job to find out who stole it and how it was done.'

'Oh!'

'I must ask you to treat the information in confidence, though I have no doubt your father will tell you the full facts later on.' He looked at the girl steadily.

'Your father wanted to tell you himself later on, but in my position I can't make a move without revealing why I want information. That being clear, might I ask if you know anybody who has an intense dislike of your father?'

'Well — er — quite a few people, really. In his business he is bound to have some enemies.'

'Just so. He has supplied me with the names of certain business people who might wish him ill. I am concerned with — shall I say, private enemies. Those disliking him for purely domestic and social reasons.'

Judith relapsed into thought. 'Only one person I can think of, but the dislike is all on daddy's side, not Jeff's . . . I'm talking about Jefferson Cole, my fiancé.'

'Yes?' Hargraves said encouragingly.

'It's nothing much, really, but daddy doesn't like Jeff — so, of course, it's mutual.'

'I see. Might I inquire the reason for this dislike?'

'Jeff isn't supposed to be good enough for me. I don't agree with that at all. If I love him — and I do — I can't see that anything else matters. After all, I want to marry him, not father.'

Hargraves rose to his feet. 'Thanks for answering my routine questions, Miss Mackinley. I'm sorry I troubled you.'

The girl hesitated over something. Hargraves waited a second or two, then seeing she did not intend to say anything further he excused himself and left the house.

4

In thoughtful mood Hargraves threaded his official car through the traffic to the Apex Garage on Morton Street and pulled up outside the main doors of the garage, away from the petrol tank runway.

Alighting from his car, he strolled casually into the garage itself and surveyed the beehive of activity.

Catching sight of him, a foreman came across. 'In trouble, sir?' he asked helpfully.

Hargraves smiled easily.

'No trouble. I'd like a word with Mr. Cole, if he's about.'

'Up there, sir. In his office.' The foreman indicated a glass-fronted structure overlooking the main floor of the repair shop. The figure of a man seated at a desk was dimly visible.

'Thanks,' Hargraves nodded, and climbed the wooden steps to the lonely retreat. As he opened the door of the office Jefferson Cole looked up with interest.

'Afternoon, sir.'

He got up expectantly from his desk and stood waiting, but the smile of welcome faded somewhat from his face as Hargraves flashed his warrant card.

'I'm Chief Inspector Hargraves, and I'd just like a few words with you,' he explained, coming forward. 'I'll not take up much of your time.'

Jeff Cole did not say anything. He levered forward a chair and then held out his cigarette case. Hargraves smiled, took one, and lit up.

'I suppose I should say 'To what do I owe the honor of this visit',' Cole murmured. 'I can't think where I've slipped up with the law. Still, I may be wrong.'

Hargraves did not say anything. Instead he studied the garage owner with a professional interest.

Jefferson Cole was handsome enough on the surface — sufficiently so to fool any romantic girl — and his voice had a polished mellowness, which was a delight to listen to. But there was something . . .

Something in the hard grey eyes, in the almost vicious set of the mouth and jaw, that didn't match up with the surface geniality.

'I could remark,' Jeff said after a while, 'that I am a very busy man, Chief Inspector.'

'Of course,' Hargraves apologized. 'Forgive my staring at you, but it's something of a professional habit I've got into . . . I'll come to the point as briefly as possible. I'm investigating a bank robbery. Fifty million pounds in gold stolen . . . from Mackinley's.'

'Mackinley's?' Jeff started slightly and his eyes widened. 'When did this happen?'

'During last night. It is not common knowledge as yet for various reasons. Mr. Mackinley is naturally reticent about allowing the public to know that his bank isn't — foolproof.'

'I should think so! A thing like that could break Mackinley!'

'I am in the midst of making routine inquiries, checking up on everybody connected with Mr. Mackinley and his private and business life. All I want from you, Mr. Cole, is a statement as to your whereabouts yesterday evening.'

Jeff sat down slowly. 'Between what times?'

'Between 7 o'clock last night and 9 o'clock this morning.'

'Let me see now. At 7 o'clock — or rather a bit before — I went to keep an appointment with Miss Mackinley at Denbey's restaurant. Afterwards we went to a play — 'Love is a Dream' — in the Haymarket. That brings us to 10.30. We went back to Denbey's at 10.30 for a little supper, leaving at 11.15. I took Miss Mackinley home in a taxi — one of my own service incidentally — and arrived at my own place toward midnight. After that I went to bed, like any other sensible person.'

'And between midnight and 7 this morning you presumably slept?'

'There's no 'presumably' about it. I did! But I can't prove it since I live alone in my flat.'

Hargraves merely nodded, giving no

indication whether he believed or disbelieved Cole's account. Then:

'Tell me, Mr. Cole — you are not on very good terms with Mr. Mackinley, are you?'

'Not particularly.' Jeff gave a shrug.

'He doesn't like me, and I don't like him. What's that got to do with it?'

Hargraves studied his cigarette end. 'The dislike, I understand, is fostered by the notion — ridiculous or otherwise — that you are not high up enough in the world for Miss Mackinley. That right?'

'That's right. But things are going to change.'

'How so?'

Jeff got up from his chair and strode purposefully to a map on the wall. He stabbed at it with a blunt forefinger.

'See that? It's a map, or rather an area plan, of the Cole Garages as they will be five years from now. Covering most of Central London, and in a position where they can't possibly miss any business. I'm even equipped for helicopter services if they come in, in a big way. In five years I shall be one of the biggest — if not the biggest — automobile men in the business.'

'This idea of yours for extensions is going to cost you plenty, Mr. Cole. Who's going to be your good fairy?'

'Mackinley.' Jeff grinned. 'Only he doesn't know it yet. I'll spring that when I've married his daughter.'

'I see . . . ' Hargraves picked up his hat. 'Well, Mr. Cole, I wish you every success with your projects, and now I'll be on my way. See you again, perhaps.'

Hargraves returned to his car, lost in thought.

★   ★   ★

After he had driven back to the Yard, Hargraves went to his office. Still frowning to himself, he sent out for sandwiches and tea, and then surveyed the notes he had made. He was in the midst of this task when Sergeant Brice came in.

'Hello, sir.' He threw his hat up on to the peg. 'Any luck in your direction?'

'Maybe. I've got to think it out first.

48

How did you make out?'

Brice gave a sigh and shrugged expressively.

'I'm afraid I haven't a thing to report, sir. More I look at this business the more baffling it gets. I've had the folks who live around the bank interrogated, and neighboring shopkeepers, but they haven't a thing to say.'

'Hmmm . . . ' Hargraves munched a sandwich mechanically. 'Which doesn't help us much. How about the big-time boys? Have you checked up on them?'

'Yes, sir. The usual evasion and politeness, but from my experience of them I'd wager they none of them had anything to do with this job. Sorry. That's the best I can do. You know I'd squeeze out information if there were any to be had.'

'Of course. Your probable failure to find anything is caused by your barking up the wrong tree. I rather think I have our man, but to hang something on him is decidedly another matter.'

'You have?' Brice sat eagerly at the desk. 'Who is it?'

'His name's Jefferson Cole, fiancé of Judith Mackinley. I may be completely wrong, mind you, but my instincts, and one or two things he let slip, lead me to think I'm on the right track.'

'What have you found out about him?'

'First, he is enormously ambitious, to the exclusion of everything else. Second, Mackinley doesn't like him because of his attentions to Judith, and I'm not surprised, having seen him.' Hargraves looked at his notes before continuing.

'When I first paid a visit to Cole this afternoon I remarked that Mackinley was naturally reticent about letting the news of the robbery leak to the public. Without hesitating, Cole replied: 'I should think so! A thing like that could break Mackinley'!'

'Which proves what exactly?' Brice asked, frowning.

'It doesn't exactly prove anything, but it shows that Cole had got the answer figured out beforehand. He must have had to grasp the implications for Mackinley so quickly. Naturally, I'm not going to pin anything on so flimsy a statement: it simply goes into the whole pattern. And the pattern as I see it is this: Jefferson Cole wants Judith Mackinley, not so much because she'll become his wife, but because she is the daughter of one of the wealthiest bankers in the country. Basic motive is not love, but money. Follow?'

'So far,' Brice acknowledged.

'Cole already owns a prosperous garage called the Apex, in Morton Street. Mackinley has said that that doesn't represent enough power and influence for the future husband of his daughter, so what does Cole do? He involves himself in tremendous garage extensions, which will stretch over a period of years, and in the end he'll possess one of the biggest automobile cum-helicopter garages in the country. But the marriage might fail completely, and Cole isn't the sort of man to involve himself in costly extensions without being sure he can pay for them. I guess at a second string to his bow — unlimited gold.'

'Or private means,' Brice said, feet on the ground as usual.

'That is possible, of course, but if he

has private means why hasn't he advertised the fact to Judith — and incidentally Mackinley — to prove that he has all the money and influence necessary to a girl of Judith's standing?'

'Yes, that's a good point,' Brice admitted.

Hargraves paused and drank his tea. Brice looked at him expectantly. 'You mean to check on him further?'

Hargraves nodded emphatically.

'Definitely. We'll check on his history, his bank, and all about him, and I'll wager we find a few surprises . . . '

Hargraves sat back in his chair.

'It's the general air of the man, his irresistible certainty of success, which intrigues me. The air, if you will, of a man who has a secret unknown to any other person on earth.'

Brice raised an eyebrow. 'The secret of shifting gold without trace?'

'Yes.'

'Then you have accepted it as a certainty that he is our man?'

'I have. Chiefly because nobody else fits the picture, and because of my personal reaction toward him. Up to now I've never guessed wrong about a man or woman in my whole career.'

Brice rose to his feet and took a turn round the office, lost in thought. Hargraves looked at his notes and reflected. After a moment the sergeant spoke again.

'Do you think there'd be anything to gain by having him in here for close questioning?'

'On what charge?' Hargraves asked bluntly. 'I can't go round picking people up for questioning just because I'm suspicious of them. I've got to have proof of what I'm doing or I'll very soon be in hot water. And until we've got something concrete — however small — we can't do a thing. Right now, the best thing we can do is find out all about Cole — his history, his education, and — if possible — his bank account.'

Brice nodded. 'I'll swing it somehow, even if I have to get the A.C. himself to make a request.'

'As for me,' Hargraves mused, 'I'm going to work out by every possible means how he could possibly have stolen all that gold without so much as a van to help him, or a single sound to give him away. I can't think of any natural means, so I'll have to try something — unnatural.'

'Unnatural?' Brice frowned.

'I was thinking of Sawley Garson. As you know, he's helped us sometimes when we've got into deep water. Remember how he helped us in the Dawson murder case recently? We'd have got nowhere without him. As an ex-government scientist he's pretty well up in odd things and scientific problems.'

'Mmmm — perhaps he'll know something,' Brice admitted. 'My personal opinion of him is that he's something of a nut. He spends his time disparaging the efforts of the Yard and saying how much better he could do the job.'

'His claim isn't altogether without justification. Don't forget his personal record, apart from being a government boffin. He's been acclaimed the Mind of Europe five times in succession in a worldwide quiz on general knowledge. That kind of a man can afford to be eccentric. Anyhow, it's worth a try. I'll do my best to see him this evening.'

5

At 5.30. Jeff Cole left his garage and headed homewards. He stayed in his flat long enough to dress himself impeccably and have a shave — then he departed again in his powerful racer, stopping at the first telephone booth he encountered.

Slipping inside the booth, he dialled the number of one of the biggest daily newspapers in the city.

'The news editor,' he requested briefly, as a voice responded.

Brief pause; then, 'News editor speaking. Can I help you?'

'I wish to remain anonymous,' Jeff said deliberately, 'but here is a piece of information which is worth a splash. Mackinley's bank was robbed last night of fifty million in gold, from a vault supposed to be foolproof. Nobody knows how it was done, and Scotland Yard is completely baffled. Mackinley himself is trying to keep the business secret, but I don't see why he should. The public needs to be told about a thing like that. Got that?'

'Yes — but I must have an address from you. There's a matter of our standard payment for your information and — '

'Quite all right. I don't want paying!'

'But don't you understand — '

Quietly, Jeff put the telephone back on its rest and smiled a little to himself, then he returned to his racer and continued his journey, finishing up at Debney's restaurant.

Judith was there at the usual table, her frank eyes smiling a welcome.

'Sorry,' Jeff apologized, sitting down. 'Just lately I always seem to be late for my appointments with you, but believe me it isn't intentional. The garage is a busy place.'

'Better busy than slack,' Judith smiled, then she paused as the waiter hovered.

Jeff gave the order and then relaxed. He looked at Judith steadily. 'Anything to tell me?' he asked after a while.

Judith raised an eyebrow. 'Such as?'

'Robbery at your father's bank, for instance.'

There was a curiously ugly look on Jeff's face that Judith had never seen before.

'Robbery? At dad's bank?'

'That's what I said. I've had the police questioning me this afternoon — and unless I'm utterly wrong they probably questioned you as well. You don't have to keep confidence with them if they ask you to, Judy. That's a lot of rubbish.'

'Well — Chief Inspector Hargraves certainly did ask me a few questions this afternoon, but he didn't get very far. What on earth could I tell him? I had nothing to do with the robbery.'

Jeff did not answer. He sat with his lips tight, keeping them pursed as the waiter arrived with the meal. Then presently as the waiter moved away he spoke again.

'You didn't, I hope, suggest that he question me?'

'Certainly not! But I did tell him of our association. That's evidently why he came to see you.'

Jeff shook his head slowly. 'He wouldn't

exert himself on an issue as trivial as that. He came to see me because your father probably suggested he should. Quite frankly, your father probably thinks I performed the robbery.'

Judith smiled a little uncertainly. 'How ridiculous!'

'It is, isn't it?'

Judith fell silent. She looked up as Jeff's hand slid across the table and grasped hers.

'Promise me something?' he asked gently.

'Of course. But what?'

'Whatever happens you'll always stick by me? There may be a lot of misunderstanding concerning me. For instance, if I suddenly start flourishing a good deal of money about in order to extend my garage, your father may — so he thinks — put two and two together. But there won't be anything in it. No connection between me and the robbery. Understand? And that's only one of the things that may happen.'

Judith smiled gently. 'You know I'll stand by you — always. As for you robbing dad's bank, the thing's impossible.'

'As you say — impossible. But consider how things might look for me. I told you yesterday that I was going to extend my garage — among other things. You may have wondered what the 'other things' might be.'

'I hadn't really thought about them.'

'But you will, m'dear. I shall use up such a lot of money that there are bound to be questions — and I'm afraid your father will ask most of them. I'm just preparing you, that's all. You know why I intend to do these things. Because in the end I intend to be more powerful and wealthy than your father could ever be.'

'I suppose so,' Judith agreed slowly, but in spite of herself she could not help but wonder what Jeff had in the back of his mind.

★ ★ ★

Sawley Garson, scientist, was unique among his class in that he knew most of the sciences inside out and yet had no impressive string of letters after his name. For this he had only himself to blame.

He maintained, not entirely without cynicism, that the teachers who set the questions did not know as much as he did. This one facet gave the clue to his whole personality — brilliant, unpredictable, and more often than not, disparaging.

He was in his small, private laboratory when Chief Inspector Hargraves called upon him that evening, and his greeting was not particularly effusive as he looked up from the chemical beaker upon which he was working.

Hargraves waited politely, doing his best to ignore the disagreeable stench of chemicals drifting round his nostrils.

'Some time since I've seen you,' Garson commented, making a note on a scratch pad. 'Not since I solved the Dawson family murder case for you. Had it not been for my intervention, the whole family might have been wiped out.'

'Uh-huh.' Hargraves didn't dispute the assertion. Indeed, he could not.

'You only come to see me when you get in deep water,' Garson added. 'Not for the charm of my company.'

He looked up fully at that — a short man with wide shoulders and a face of unusually dogged qualities. The nose was hooked, the jaw square, and the eyes two sapphire needle points, which glinted from beneath bushy eyebrows. Most dominant of all was the forehead — an upsweeping cliff topped by a disordered mass of sandy hair.

'I freely confess I'm in a bit of a fog,' Hargraves sighed, settling on a stool.

'So you come to the professional fog-disperser — Sawley Garson. Well, what is it this time?'

'Bank robbery on the grand scale.'

'At Mackinley's Bank? I haven't taken time to read all the facts,' Garson said, sucking at his pipe, 'but I did notice the headlines in tonight's paper.'

'But — but you can't have read about it! There's been a close clamp on all information.'

The scientist shrugged. 'Then your information must have leaked — ' He began moving. 'Come to think of it, I brought the rag here, so I — Ah, here it is!'

He yanked up the issue in question from under a pile of newly planted papers and handed it over.

Hargraves looked at it grimly, then his eye traveled to the 'Late Final Edition' caption in the right-hand corner. The headlines were certainly impressive — and to the point:

'Mackinley's Bank Robbed of Fifty Million.'

In silence Hargraves read the rest of the information. It was all there, even to the point of saying that Scotland Yard did not know which way to turn. Savagely Hargraves slapped the paper down.

'I'd give my job to know who spilt this news!' he snapped. 'It was supposed to be secret. Mackinley will climb up the wall when he finds out.'

'An acrobatic feat I would love to see. But you said you wanted my help?' Garson smoked placidly and waited.

'Maybe you'd better read what the newspaper says about it.'

'I can't be bothered. Give me the facts yourself.'

Hargraves did so, with great attention to detail, including the more baffling points, which were not in the paper.

Garson listened, dragging at his pipe, and remained completely silent when Hargraves had finished his story.

'Very interesting,' he said presently. 'Very, very interesting.'

'As I tell you, I suspect young Jefferson Cole. It's more or less working on a hunch, but usually when I play my hunches they come off.'

'If he's your man, have you tried to figure out where he's put all that gold?' Garson asked. 'Have you searched his garage?'

'I can't do that without getting a search-warrant, and at the moment I've insufficient evidence.'

Garson relit his pipe. 'I can pick on only one slender clue in the whole set-up, and it's probably a clue of which the perpetrator never thought.'

'What's that?'

'The watchman's radio. Didn't you say

he was trying no listen to the singing from the Albert Hall, but couldn't because of interference?'

'That's his story.'

'And yet you listened to it at home without trouble? Did I get that right?'

'Quite right.' Hargraves agreed. 'The wife's rather partial to good music, so we had that radio program instead of watching the usual television. But what are you driving at?'

'Simply that the interference was not from the station, nor apparently was it atmospheric. It was something local. Before we go any further we'd better check on people owning a radio or television in the vicinity of Mackinley's bank. Even the police should be able to find such people.'

Hargraves looked genuinely puzzled. He seemed unaware of the sarcasm. 'We can do that easily enough, of course — but what's the idea?'

'Simply this. If something electrical was used to vanish the gold it would upset all radios — and television sets — within the area. That's child's play. Satisfy ourselves on that, then perhaps we know what we're driving at. You'll do that?'

'Just a minute! Aren't you forgetting the bank's own tv pictures? PC Harkins told me there was nothing wrong with them — they gave uninterrupted images from inside the bank all through the night.'

'I never forget anything!' Garson snorted. 'The bank's cameras operate on a closed-circuit — nothing to do with broadcast transmissions. Entirely different matter. They'd be unaffected unless they were interfered with physically.'

Hargraves rose to his feet and reached for his hat.

'Right! I'll be with you again the moment I've got the information we want.'

With that he went on his way, reflecting on the number of things he had to do.

For one thing he had to discover who had let the cat out of the bag regarding Mackinley's bank — a point upon which he sensed Mackinley would be particularly sore.

He was right.

The night edition had hit Mackinley in the eye as he had been leaving home, It did not take him long to get the news editor on the phone.

'I'm Mackinley!' Mackinley said grimly. 'Owner of the Mackinley bank. Who gave you the information that there had been a robbery at my bank?'

'Frankly, sir, we don't know,' the news editor replied. 'He wouldn't give his name — '

'So it was a man?'

'Without doubt. If the statement was false it can be retracted, with apologies. Otherwise it's too good a story to miss.'

Mackinley put the phone down again, then he put a series of names down on the blotter and considered each one carefully.

'Nobody at the bank would do a thing like that because whatever happens to the bank will rebound on the staff, so they'd keep shut up. Certainly the Yard wouldn't break confidence either. That leaves only one man — that confounded upstart Jeff Cole. He must know about the business if Chief Inspector Hargraves has called and questioned him. So help me, I'll settle this for once and for all!'

His cigar speared arrogantly between his lips, he left the study and strode into the lounge. His wife, lazily reading, glanced up at him in surprise.

'Anything the matter, Joe?' she asked curiously.

'Plenty! Where's Judy?'

'I thought you knew . . . She's out as usual with young Jeff Cole.'

Mackinley sat down and pointed his cigar emphatically. 'He's informed the 'Sentinel' that a robbery has occurred at the bank.'

'Well, it would be bound to come out sooner or later, wouldn't it? Incidentally how do you know it was Jeff?'

'It's a logical inference and it's also the last straw.' Mackinley stubbed his cigar savagely into the brass ashtray fixed in a leather strap across the arm of his chair.

'I'm going to do what I should have done long ago: I am going to stop Judith having any further association with him!'

'Probably Judy will have something to say about that,' Ethel Mackinley smiled.

'This time I won't listen to her. I never did like the fellow — '

Mackinley stopped as the lounge door opened and Judith herself came in, still in her outdoor things.

The magnate frowned towards her; then his face colored deeply as behind Judith there came the slimly elegant figure of Jeff Cole himself, smiling in that curiously hard way he had.

'Hello, mum, dad.' Judith tripped lightly forward, pulling off her gloves. 'Well, come in, Jeff!' she added, laughing. 'Don't just stand there! You know the place well enough.'

'What's the meaning of this?' Mackinley demanded suddenly, looking at Judith. 'How dare you bring this — this man here?'

'She didn't,' Jeff said calmly. 'In fact it was the other way about. I wanted to tell you personally, in Judy's company, that we have decided to be married in a month's time.'

'May I be the first — ' Ethel Mackinley started to say, but her husband cut her short.

'Don't speak too soon, Ethel! I'm dead against this marriage as I was dead against the engagement! I won't have it!'

'If Judy were under age you could enforce your will, of course,' Jeff smiled, 'but as it is — '

'Don't you tell me what I can do and what I can't do, Cole!' Mackinley heaved himself to his feet. He glared at Jeff as he stood smiling faintly.

'At the present moment I'm aware of only one thing — You're in my house, and I don't like it!'

'What's Jeff done, anyway?' Judith blazed suddenly, her eyes flashing. 'Do you have to be so unreasonable?'

'Yes, I do! And it isn't unreasonable.' Mackinley breathed bard and then looked at Jeff squarely. 'Answer me one question, Cole. Why did you think it necessary to inform the 'Sentinel' of the robbery at my bank?'

Jeff stared. 'Why did I what?'

'I suppose you're going to deny it?'

'With all respect, Mr. Mackinley, I don't know what you're talking about.'

'I expected you'd say that,' Mackinley

snapped. 'That action confirms my earlier belief about you. I don't like you, and I never did, and I'll not have my daughter associating with you. Now will you kindly leave?'

Jeff tightened his lips. 'You leave me no option since this is your house, Mr. Mackinley — but if you think this will make the least difference between Judith and I you're vastly mistaken; Good night!'

With that he swung on his heel, reached the door, and was gone. For one moment Judith stared after him and half moved, until her father's hand flashed out and seized her arm.

'No you don't, Judy! Let him go!'

'In the circumstances I can't help it!' she retorted. 'But it's time you realized, dad, that you have no power to control my life at my age. I intend to marry Jeff, and that's that.'

'Now listen to me, Judy — '

'Sorry, but I'd rather not.' She grabbed her father's restraining arm and glared at him. Reluctantly, he released his grip.

The girl rushed towards the door. Opening it, she looked over her shoulder to where her father still stood, rigid with anger. Tersely, she said:

'I've got to catch up with Jeff and try somehow to apologize for your appalling behavior towards him.'

Rushing outside, she found Jeff in his car, just about to pull away. As she called out to him, he switched off the engine and waited.

'You'll have to forgive dad, Jeff,' Judith insisted gently, as she slipped into the front seat beside him. 'He gets that way at times, and probably this bank business has made it worse. I don't think he meant half of what he said.'

'If he didn't, he made a convincing job of it! I'll tell you one thing — I shan't even mention to him again that we're going to be married. We'll just bypass him. Sorry, Judy: I know he's your father, but that's how I feel.'

'Frankly, I don't blame you — but I'll talk him round at an opportune moment.' Judith glanced quickly at her watch. 'It's not so late yet. How about a drive round?'

'I — er,' Jeff paused and looked apologetic.

'Afraid I can't. I've got to turn in at the garage and do one or two things.'

'Any reason why your future wife can't come with you? The air in the house is liable to be a bit stormy.'

'There's nothing I'd like better only — Well, to be blunt, I don't think it's a good idea to mix women and business.'

'I see.' Her nerves already pretty strained after the events of the evening, Judith found this observation nearly too much. Her mouth set she opened the door and climbed out into the drive.

'You do understand, Judy, surely?' Jeff asked anxiously.

'Of course.' Her voice was cool. 'Same place, same time, tomorrow night? Or have you garage work to do?'

'I shan't have tomorrow. Same place — same time.'

Judith nodded, ignored all Jeff's invitations to a goodnight kiss, and went off up the drive. For a moment or two Jeff watched her in the dim light, then with a scowl on his face he started up the engine of his racer and sped out into the roadway.

6

At 9 o'clock next morning Chief Inspector Hargraves was already in his dingy office in Whitehall when Sergeant Harry Brice arrived. Brice immediately cleared his throat and endeavored to think up an excuse for his own slight unpunctuality.

Morning, sir,' he greeted, hanging up his hat.

'Morning . . . ' If Hargraves realized Brice was late he gave no sign of it. Instead he studied his notes intently: then he raised an eyebrow. 'Take a look at that!'

Brice looked — and gave a start. It was a message that had been received, and acted upon, during the night. It stated briefly:

Report by Supt. Maddison. For Insp. Hargraves. Summoned at 1.30 a.m. to home of Joseph Mackinley to investigate the sudden death of Joseph Mackinley. No suspicion of foul play. Heart failure.

Surgeon's report and my own report attached. Maddison.

'Mackinley's dead!' Brice exclaimed, astounded.

'Yes — Mackinley himself. Maddison was just going off duty when I arrived, so I had a few words with him. Lucky that various things brought me here earlier than usual . . . It seems Mackinley had a severe heart attack in the night and died almost immediately.'

'It's confoundedly unexpected,' Brice said, thinking.

'Naturally, this makes no difference to the business we're engaged upon,' Hargraves continued, 'though it will make it rather harder without our being able to call on Mackinley for this or that piece of information. Anyway — to business. I saw Sawley Garson last night, and he's interested.'

'Good!'

'Interested — with reservations. He won't touch the job until I supply him with certain information — namely, how were the radios and televisions behaving in the vicinity of the bank the night before last, when the robbery was committed. Well, I spent most of last evening checking up and then went on home.'

'What did you find, sir?'

'I found,' Hargraves said slowly, 'that all radios and televisions in the immediate area had severe interference between 10 and 10.45 p.m. Then it ceased as suddenly as it had commenced. It seems it was impossible to hear or see any programme.'

'In other words, something highly electrical in the area?'

'Precisely. That's the information which Garson wants, though what he proposes to make out of it I can't imagine. He also suggested that we investigate Jefferson Cole thoroughly and try and figure out where he put fifty million in gold blocks when he took it — if he took it.'

Hargraves paused and glanced through his notes, then: 'I left you with directions yesterday. To find out all about him and, if possible, contact his bank. How did you make out?'

'I've still to contact his bank, sir, during business hours. Too late yesterday. I'll do it this morning. However, I spent last night around the district where he lives — apparently as a casual visitor to the district. I made discreet inquiries about him, particularly of men engaged in the motor business.'

'Well? What did you find out?'

'Quite a lot. On the whole he doesn't seem to be generally liked. Also he has a lot of high-flown ambitions. Particularly interesting, I thought, was the information that he was once at Oxford, where he took several degrees in science.'

'Several?'

'If he wanted he could have become a doctor of science or a doctor of physics, but he turned them down in favor of becoming a garage owner.'

Hargraves got to his feet. 'Well, I'd better see what Garson has to say for himself now I've got the information he wanted. You had better do what you can to sort out Cole's bank account.'

'I'll do that, sir, somehow.'

Hargraves nodded and went on his way.

Within a very short time Hargraves was at Sawley Garson's home once more — and as usual he found him in the midst of chemical experiments in the laboratory.

'Hello, Hargraves!' Garson glanced up and laid a test tube on one side. 'Resumption of the bad penny, I presume?'

'You can call it that — and I've some fresh information for you which will very quickly hit the newspapers. Joseph Mackinley died in the night — from a heart attack.'

'Did he now? Heart attack, you say? Quite sure?'

'In my own mind, no — but what can I do against medical evidence?'

'I see what you mean.' Garson tugged out his briar and thumbed tobacco into the bowl. 'Well, did you find out what I wanted to know?'

'I did. Spent all evening on it. All radios and televisions in the vicinity of Mackinley's bank suffered severe interference between 10 o'clock and 10.45 on the night of the robbery.'

'Splendid! That gives us a working basis and sorts out the first point. Something electrical caused the disappearance of the gold between 10 and 10.45.'

Hargraves smiled tiredly. 'Sounds interesting, but what on earth, in the electrical line, could commit the robbery?'

'That's what we have to find out — probably by a long and arduous route. The first thing we have to do is discover if Cole — if you are still sure he's your man — has any unusual electrical equipment.'

Hargraves reflected. 'Even if he has, he won't be ass enough to have it where anybody can see it. He wouldn't, for instance, keep anything like that at his garage.'

'Since we don't want him to suspect special attention, the thing to do is draw him into the open — and at the same time test my own theory,' Garson said at length. 'You say he's ambitious?'

'No doubt of it.'

'Ambitious enough to try and steal

another fortune if he knew it was there for the taking?'

Hargraves frowned. 'How do you mean?'

'I want to test a theory — the electrical one. For that we need bait. Do you think you could get Mackinley's bank to put out the story that another big gold consignment is being handled by them to replace the gold that has been stolen?'

'This is all relying on the fact that Cole becomes ambitious enough to try again.' Hargraves said. 'Supposing he smells a rat?'

'In that case we'll try something else, but an ambitious man takes notorious risks and I don't see any reason why our criminal friend shouldn't run true to type. You see to it, and let me know when the arrangements are made.'

Hargraves did not ask any more questions: it was not good policy with a man like Sawley Garson.

Puzzled, but willing to obey orders he departed and drove to Mackinley's bank.

On the surface everything was the same as usual, but when he asked to see the person who had taken authority in Mackinley's place, he was particularly surprised to discover none other than Judith Mackinley in the luxurious private office.

'Good morning, Miss Mackinley.' Hargraves removed his hat and shook the girl's hand as she rose from the desk to greet him.

'You are about the last person I expected to see.'

'Very probably.' The girl gave a rather despondent smile. 'For the moment — and maybe permanently if the board of directors agree — I am the official head of the bank. Dad wished it that way.'

'I see. And while I am about it may I express my sincere sympathy for what happened?'

'Thank you, Mr. Hargraves. Naturally, it was a terrible shock for all of us, but as far as I personally am concerned I have got over the worst. I'm here because dad said I had to be. He left written orders to that effect.'

'Oh?' Hargraves looked surprised. 'At home, you mean? His will can't — '

'No, no. His will hasn't been proven yet, of course. He left a sealed letter here at the bank stating what was to happen if sudden death overtook him. As a result of that letter I find myself completely in his mantle as his daughter. I suppose he should have preferred a son in the position, but I'll do my best.'

'I'm sure you will.'

'There's a meeting of the directors later this morning.' the girl added, returning thoughtfully to her chair at the desk. 'Then we can arrange things.'

As Hargraves hesitated, Judith smiled faintly.

'I'm sorry,' she apologized. 'Naturally you didn't come here just to find out who was operating in father's place. Is there something I can do for you?'

'There is — in regard to the robbery.'

Hargraves sat down and thought for a moment, then: 'We have discovered quite a deal, Miss Mackinley, but we're still a little bogged down by our inability to drag the culprit into the open. So, we plan a trap.'

Judith nodded. 'I understand. Does the

bank come into it?'

'Very much so. This is what we hope to do . . . ' and Hargraves outlined the scheme in detail.

Judith listened attentively, her expression giving no clue as to what she was thinking. When he had finished Hargraves looked at her hopefully.

Judith shrugged, 'Very well, Mr. Hargraves, it's all right as far as I am concerned. I'll see Mr. Burton, the head cashier, and arrange it with him. He'll advise the newspapers. As for the board of directors, I'll have to invent something for them — or does it matter if they know it's a trick?'

'Tell them the truth,' Hargraves said. 'Then there'll be no slip-ups. They know about the robbery, so they might as well know what efforts are being made to solve the business.'

Judith nodded. 'Is there any time limit, or shall we say as soon as possible?'

'Make it the day after tomorrow. Tell the press for tomorrow. The quicker action we take the quicker we'll be in finding the culprit. And not a word to anybody outside those immediately concerned.'

'Very well . . . Judith's attention seemed to wander for a moment: then she forced herself back to the matter on hand. 'Is there anything more, inspector?'

'I don't think so . . . ' Hargraves hesitated. He gave the girl a direct look.

'Forgive me, Miss Mackinley, but have you got something on your mind?'

'As a matter of fact I have. You can call it the imaginings of a young woman if you like, but to me it's something more than that.'

She leaned forward suddenly across the desk, entirely confidential in her manner.

'I think, despite every evidence to the contrary, that my father was murdered! Don't ask me how, or by whom, but I cannot get away from the belief.'

'What makes you think so?'

'It seems so impossible for dad to suddenly have a heart attack of sufficient severity to kill him. A mild one I might have credited at his age, and particularly with so much worry on his mind at the moment — but beyond that I can't

84

believe. Even less so when Dr. Calhoun — that's our family practitioner — gave him a clean bill of health less than a fortnight ago.'

'He did?' Hargraves looked surprised. 'If you have any doubts at all there ought to be an inquest.'

Judith gestured vaguely. 'On what grounds can I possibly base my suspicions? It's purely my own imagining.' She reflected for a moment and then shook her head.

'No, let it be,' she said quietly. 'No use stirring up trouble without being sure of one's ground.'

7

When she had sorted things out as well as she could with the board of directors, and secured their agreement to Joseph Mackinley's wish that she herself should assume presidency of the bank, Judith set into operation the scheme which Hargraves had described to her.

At first the idea had been accepted in dubious silence, until by steady insistence Judith had succeeded in gaining her object — permission generally to launch the scheme. This done the rest was up to Burton, the head cashier.

So, feeling that she had accomplished all that was required of her for the moment, Judith returned home in somewhat better spirits.

The only thing she regretted was that, in view of bereavement upon the family, it was necessary for her out of good taste to cancel her usual social activities — Jeff Cole included . . . Not to be outdone, however, he arrived in the evening about 7.30 to find Judith alone in the lounge.

'Hello, Jeff!' she greeted, rising from the divan and kissing him. 'I was wondering if you'd come.'

'Wondering, were you? Was it for a moment ever in doubt? Ever since you phoned me during the night that your dad had passed away I've been anxious to get to you, and console you. But as usual business kept me chained.'

'Sit down,' Judith said, motioning. 'I'm so glad to have you here, to take my mind off things.'

Jeff seated himself, putting his arm about Judith's shoulders as she settled beside him.

'About last evening,' he said slowly. 'We parted in rather a huff. Although tragedy made you ring me up in the night, I was rather glad of it. Sort of set my mind at rest that you're still my girl.'

'Well, of course I am! And don't you ever doubt it.'

Cole looked about him, frowning slightly.

'Where's your mother, by the way?'

'Resting. The shock of what's happened has laid her pretty low.'

'I can imagine,' Jeff nodded sympathetically. 'And you? Still bearing up?'

'Oh, yes. Matter of fact I've had so much to do at the bank I haven't had much time to dwell on my own troubles.'

Jeff turned his head slowly. 'Busy at the bank? What on earth concern is the bank of yours?'

'Every concern now dad is dead. I've taken his place as the president. If that sounds grandiloquent, it simply means that I am the figurehead and the trained staff does all the rest.'

'I see.' Jeff smiled ironically. 'Congratulations, Madam President.'

Judith smiled a little; nothing more. 'I hope my becoming the president of the bank won't in any way affect our relationship. Will you feel up to marrying such a person?'

'It makes not the least difference . . . I can easily match you in importance, or at least I will do before long.'

Judith gave an odd, half quizzical glance. 'You say the strangest things, Jeff.

Sometimes I think I don't understand you one little bit.'

'Sorry.' Jeff spread his hands. 'My nature and ambitions are easily summed up. First comes you, and second comes money. Those are my only two interests . . . ' His mood changed abruptly.

'Isn't it rather marvelous that I can be sitting here without stirring up opposition? So different to last evening.'

'So different.' Judith agreed, sighing. 'If only dad had seen things in the proper light . . . if only he had! You're perfectly welcome to come here whenever you wish, Jeff — you know that. Mother is entirely in favor of you.'

'Good old mother!' Jeff grinned; then his expression slowly changed. 'That reminds me! Now your father's gone, how's the Yard going to handle the bank robbery business?'

'Oh, they're still at it. As a matter of fact I saw Chief Inspector Hargraves today. Now that I've taken dad's place they address all their questions to me.'

'I can't think what questions they can have to ask. Why the devil don't they get on with finding the thief instead of just playing around with questions? More I see of the Yard the more I think it needs some trained brains in charge of it.'

'I don't think Chief Inspector Hargraves is a fool, by any means. He may be quiet in manner — but then all British inspectors usually are. Matter of fact — '

'Well?' Jeff asked casually, as Judith hesitated.

She gave him a direct look. Faintly arrogant grey eyes looked steadily back at her.

'After all, I suppose as my future husband you're in the immediate circle,' she mused.

Jeff sighed. 'Would you mind being a bit more explicit?'

'Just trying to settle something in my mind.' Judith still hesitated, then she plunged.

'All right then, here it is! Since you don't think the Yard's doing much, listen to their latest . . . ' and she went into the full details of the gold 'bait' that had been devised.

Jeff smiled. 'We'll have to see what happens.'

8

And while this tête-à-tête was progressing in the Mackinley residence, Chief Inspector Hargraves was at work in his office.

He had not gone home at the usual time — neither had Sergeant Brice. There was a good deal of recapitulation to be gone through, a lot of bits and pieces to be drawn together and sewn up neat and tight.

Only by degrees was Chief Inspector Hargraves commencing to realize that here he had a case that was not going to be easy to crack.

'The robbery.' he said, glancing at Brice, 'took place between 10 and 10.45. That much we have established, providing something electrical brought it about. It was during that time that electrical interference was set in motion. Right! Our suspicions are on Jefferson Cole because he fits the bill better than anybody. What was his alibi for that night?'

'Rather a difficult one — for us,' Brice said gloomily, looking at the notes. 'Cole was with Judith Mackinley at those times — first seeing a play in the Haymarket and then going to Debney's for supper at 10.30, leaving around 11.15. He couldn't have done a bank robbery and been with Judith at the same time.'

'No.' Hargraves tightened his lips and stared in front of him. 'No — he couldn't. Unless . . . '

'Unless what?'

'If something electrical was used it might have been remote controlled — just the same as an electric stove. For instance, you can set an electric stove — the oven anyway — to reduce itself to a certain temperature at a certain time, and then go out and leave it.'

'Yes. I suppose so, but — ' Brice scratched his head. 'What on earth kind of device could it be that robs a bank and allows the inventor to go out with his girl friend while it happens? Just think what you could do with a contrivance like that!'

'There's another side to this matter yet,' Hargraves went on. 'Far more serious than the robbery, though that's bad enough in all conscience. I'm talking about — murder.'

'Is this a fact, sir, or assumption?'

'Assumption — which often arises yelling out for an answer. It has become a stronger assumption since Miss Mackinley told me that she thinks her father was somehow murdered.'

'Oh? Does she?' The sergeant's eyebrows rose. 'On what grounds?'

'A fortnight ago, Harry, Dr. Calhoun — the family physician — gave Mackinley the okay for health. Not a thing wrong with him, for a man of his age. Then suddenly — phut! Out like a light.'

'Probably the bank robbery preyed on his mind.'

'I dunno,' Hargraves mused. 'But if a man can rob a bank and go out with his girl friend at the same time, he might be capable of other things . . . I think a little firsthand information from Dr. Calhoun is called for.'

Hargraves reached for the telephone, and after a while he succeeded in contacting Calhoun. Fortunately he had just finished surgery for the evening and could give his full attention.

'Yes, yes,' he assented, as Hargraves identified himself. 'You have the facts straight, Chief Inspector. I gave Mr. Mackinley a clean bill of health two weeks ago.'

'Then, normally, nothing could have caused his death?'

'I am wondering if perhaps his general attitude during the evening might not have brought on heart failure: it could, in a man of his age.'

'General attitude?' Hargraves repeated, interested. 'Why, what happened?'

'Perhaps you don't know the details. Judith gave them to me when I was making a few inquiries. Mr. Mackinley had been in a towering temper most of the evening — first because the news of the robbery at his bank had been made public; and second because a Mr. Cole had arrived with Judith during the evening, saying he was going to marry her. I gather this started a violent scene.'

Hargraves' eyes narrowed. 'I see — and

thank you for the information. I was unaware of it.'

Hargraves put the telephone back on its cradle. He did not need to tell Brice what Calhoun had said: he had heard it clearly enough in the receiver.

'Well,' Brice said, 'that seems more or less to finish it. Mackinley got worked up because of two things, worked up to such an extent that he died.'

'Yes — about 1 in the morning, long after his rage must have cooled off!' Hargraves gave a grim look. 'Pretty long distance between rage and the death, if you ask me. All the cases I have ever heard of produce death, or a severe stroke, at the height of the rage — not after it has subsided.'

'And how was the murder — if it was murder — committed?' Brice insisted.

'I don't know. Garson might. I'll put it to him.'

Hargraves glanced at his watch. 'Close on 9. I think we might stroll over and take a look at Cole's garage — without attracting anybody's attention, that is.'

'Okay. For what reason?'

'I'm following out Garson's suggestion to try to figure out where the gold went to. It must be somewhere — yet we don't want to excite Cole's suspicions. Let's go — without the car.'

Together they set off to walk the short distance to the Apex Garage. Once within sight of it they slowed down, surveying the busy activity of cars and trucks coming and going along the ramps leading to the filling pumps. There was plenty of business here but the garage proper was closed.

'Those must be the extensions,' Hargraves murmured, nodding to a big area contiguous to the garage where steel scaffolding had been erected.

Brice nodded. 'Doesn't seem to be anybody around, either. We might as well take a look.'

They moved on again, studying the garage and extensions from every angle — and learning exactly nothing. They passed a tar-mixing machine, with a great tower of tar bricks beside it. They passed a cement mixer, a concrete layer, and several other articles connected with the building — but these told them nothing.

Then as they were coming around the corner which separated them from the garage itself they were startled by a sudden voice.

'Hello, boys! Taking the air?'

Hargraves twirled. He and Brice stood looking at a short man in a big overcoat strolling toward them. He had very wide shoulders, and a short pipe was glowing menacingly.

'Garson, as I live and breathe!' Hargraves exclaimed in relief. 'What on earth are you doing here?'

'Just looking,' the scientist grinned. 'There are times when I come up for air, you know, and this is one of them. I suppose you two are taking a constitutional? Being after hours?'

'I'll come right to the point,' Hargraves said gruffly. 'We're looking for a possible place where the gold bricks from Mackinley's might have been stored.'

'And you expect to find them here?'

'Not really. We're just surveying the size and extent of the alterations Cole intends to make.'

'Hmmm — let's get down to more important things. If you had to store something extremely valuable, and wanted to hide it from everybody, would you choose a safe? Or an obvious place?'

'Come to think of it, I wouldn't. I'd probably put it somewhere obvious. So obvious that nobody would think anything about it.'

'I observe,' Garson said calmly, 'that the brains of the Yard are still well polished. But maybe I've gone one further — perhaps because I got here before you. For instance, try these for weight.'

He didn't explain there and then. Instead he started walking, and frowning deeply, Hargraves and Brice followed him. They stopped again finally beside the tar bricks intended for the tar-mixing machine.

'Well?' Hargraves asked, mystified — and Garson motioned to the tar bricks.

'Try one.'

Puzzled, Hargraves did so. He seized the topmost brick and then gasped at its heaviness.

'What's the answer, Garson?' he asked.

'An incredible one, but I think it's quite true. I think these tar blocks were once gold, and can become so again when necessary.'

Hargraves did not know whether to laugh or burst into fury. While he measured his emotions, Garson went on talking.

'No genius of mine led me to these tar blocks. I simply raised one experimentally as I passed, and its tremendous weight led me to a chain of reasoning. Before I explain further, though, just notice where these tar blocks and the tar-making machine are standing.'

Hargraves and Brice both looked, but failed to see anything significant.

'To put it briefly,' the scientist continued, 'this tar-making machine is nowhere near the building operations. More concisely, I don't think it's being used by the builders anyway. It's for something else.'

'It's queer,' Hargraves said at last. 'Darned queer.'

'It's a matter of weight and transmutation of elements,' the scientist explained.

'If that gold were somehow converted into sugar it would still retain the same atomic weight, even though it would look like sugar: In this case I believe the gold has been transmutated into tar — or some element that looks like it — but one cannot escape the basic weight. I'll wager that one of these blocks, if weighed, would be exactly equivalent to a block of gold of the same weight.'

'You talk very casually about transmutation of elements.' Hargraves said. 'Isn't that an impossible alchemy?'

'By no means. It is done today in many of the modern laboratories, but not on any great scale. The method received a tremendous impetus upon the discovery of atomic secrets. I can even do it myself on a limited scale, but I'm short of a catalyst.'

'Short of a what?' Hargraves asked rather dully

'A catalyst. That is an x-factor, an unknown quantity in chemistry, which produces an unusual effect upon a known formula. For instance, changing elements would be ridiculously easy if we could happen on the right catalyst, either by accident or design. I'm suggesting that, apart from other scientific discoveries, our friend Cole has found a transmutation catalyst — and he's using it to good effect.'

Hargraves, a down-to-earth police officer, began to realize that he was getting into deep water. But then, he might have expected it as far as Sawley Carson was concerned.

'If what you suggest is right,' Brice said, pondering, 'it defeats its own object. If Cole has the ability to transform things into gold, or vice versa, why did he bother to rob the bank? He could have manufactured the gold out of — of old iron, or something.'

'But he wouldn't have encompassed Mackinley's possible ruin,' said Hargraves. 'Cole's object wasn't only to rob the bank and give it a dubious name, but also to enjoy the thrill of getting it out of the bank into the bargain . . . Still no idea how he did that, Garson?'

'Of course I've an idea, but it wants working on. I'm doing that at the lab right now . . . I think,' Garson went on, 'that in Cole we have a remarkably clever and dangerous man.'

'I guessed that from the first,' Hargraves growled. 'What do you suppose I ought to do? Take these tar bricks?'

'And give things away? The moment these vanish, Cole will know you're up to something, and that will make the job harder for both of us.'

'But I can't let him keep these bricks! If he decides to convert them back into gold, what then?'

'I don't think he will — yet. He'll prefer to be more certain of his ground first. Maybe when the hue and cry is off.' A humorous twinkle came into Garson's eyes.

'And I'd remind you of something, Hargraves. If you start hawking these tar bricks along to the forensic laboratory you're liable to get yourself certified. You don't suppose any normal chemist or analyst would believe your story that these bricks are really gold, do you?'

Hargraves reflected. 'I'd have your word, besides my own. That would count for a good deal. Even at a pinch you could convert these things back, into their original form perhaps?'

'I couldn't — not without the catalyst. That's Cole's secret. Quite frankly, Hargraves, you can't do a thing yet. We know what's going on, but we can't prove anything. Which gives Cole his tremendous advantage. Galling though it is, we'll have to leave things exactly as they are — for the moment. Stick around,' Garson added, 'and I'll see if I can find out a thing or two.'

Hargraves and Brice stood watching as Garson went across to his car in one of the nearby side streets. He drove it directly to the petrol pump ramp, and there he sat for quite a while in earnest conversation.

Together they reached the street and prepared to wait. It was not long before Garson's car appeared around the bend. He stopped and opened the door for the two men to get in.

'I'll run you back to the Yard,' he explained. 'If that's where you're going?'

'Do that,' Hargraves nodded, as the

car moved on. 'And what did you find out?'

'Enough to satisfy us for the moment, anyhow. Cole is very soon going to have fresh tar and macadam put on the garage runways, and those blocks and the tar-mixer are for that purpose. He hasn't said when he's going to do it, or who's going to do the job — so I think we can take it that the whole thing is a blind. The tar machine is solely for the purpose of taking attention from the tar blocks. And they're far enough away from the extension site not to be used by those builders.'

'Cole's taking a mighty big risk,' Brice commented; but Garson shook his head.

'I don't think he is. On the contrary, I think he is being rather smart. Nobody in a million years will suspect those tar blocks as meaning anything — and he can leave them there as long as he likes, until the time comes for restoring them to normal and getting rid of them.'

'There's a point, and a big one,' Hargraves said. 'Where does he do all this scientific jiggery pokery? We haven't the least clue.'

'Not so far, and it's a waste of time trying to find his hideout. That will come when he acts — probably during the second gold consignment. I'll have detectors that will show us the point of origin of his electrical interference. Then we'll get somewhere. You managed to fix that business by the way?'

'Yes,' Hargraves nodded. 'The consignment will be the day after tomorrow. Tomorrow will be used for spreading the news in the press. I was going to ring you up about it.'

'Just as long as I know. I'll be ready.'

Garson threaded his way through the traffic and then drew in to the curb as Scotland Yard was reached.

'I'll keep you posted,' he said, as Hargraves prepared to get out. 'You've done your part: now it's up to me.'

Hargraves and Brice nodded and climbed out of the car; then as they turned into the Yard's gloomy reaches they looked at each other.

'Found a good deal more than we

expected, sir,' Brice commented. 'Gold bricks disguised as tar is a new one on me.'

'A new one on anybody, I'll gamble,' Hargraves growled. 'And as I said before, it's not so much this present case that has me worried as what may happen in the future.'

'The future?'

'A man who's got a secret like Cole has can do anything — and get away with it. Our only hope is Garson when it comes to the technical side. As far as routine police work goes, we've about exhausted our resources.'

Hargraves opened the office door and, as he walked in, added: 'By the way, I've had so many things on my mind I neglected to ask you what you did find out about Cole's bank account?'

'Nothing,' Brice shrugged. 'I couldn't get the bank manager to divulge any information — not without any concrete reason for wanting it.'

'Hmmm — might have expected it. I know you've got to have very strong reasons. Not that it matters much now since Cole has not added anything to his bank account from the gold he's stolen. That much we know . . . All right, forget it . . . '

9

The following evening, when the first editions of the papers were on the streets, Brice went for a copy of all the papers that mattered.

In each one he and Hargraves between them found some reference — big or little, according to the editor's estimate of its value — to the proposed gold 'consignment' to the Mackinley Bank the following day. This time there was to be £2,000,000 worth, well worth any crook's attention.

Yes — everything was nicely set, and toward 5.30 Sawley Garson rang up to say that he had read the papers and wanted to meet Hargraves and Brice at the bank itself the following morning.

Though they had no real idea of what the scientist was doing, they duly presented themselves at the bank just after opening time the following morning.

On the surface, it appeared business

was proceeding as usual. The two men were shown into a private office, where Garson was already installed, smoking contentedly, a big mahogany box with a hinged lid by his side.

'Morning, boys,' he greeted, sucking at his pipe. Feeling merry and bright?'

'Does one ever, in this business?' Hargraves growled, and Garson grinned widely.

'Never mind. I think what is going to happen this time will wreath your face in sunbeams. Right here,' — he stabbed a finger toward the mahogany box — 'is a Garson electronic detector. You won't find it in any store, but you might find a somewhat similar gadget in certain hush-hush quarters of the air ministry. In a less sensitive form it is used by the Air Ministry for detection of frequencies from enemy aircraft and what-have-you. Now I have modified it. It will show in a moment the direction from which any kind of electronic wave is coming — pinpointing it to within half a mile. After that we should be able to do something.'

'Uh-huh,' Hargraves agreed, unaccountably edgy.

'Burton's in charge of everything,' Garson added. 'The arrival of the phony gold is set for 10.30. By 11.30 it ought to be in the vault. Then it will be locked in. and us with it.'

Hargraves started. 'Us with it?'

'Well, of course! You want to see the good old clay bricks do a vanishing act, don't you? It should be phenomenal to see it happen! The vault door will be left ajar so we can get out in case of sudden emergency. Nothing will happen before evening, I don't suppose, so we'll have quite a time to wait. The bank staff hasn't been told what is going on, but they have been warned that certain developments are afoot ... We can send out for sandwiches and tea,' Garson added casually.

Hargraves gave Brice a glance, and the sergeant grimaced.

'For myself, sir, I'd sooner have a good old-fashioned knife murder! At least we'd know what we're doing.'

'Regarding your side of the business,'

Garson resumed. 'What have you done, Hargraves?'

'I've made arrangements for a detail of men to supervise the unloading of the 'gold' at the bank here; and I've got some of my best men keeping a watch on Cole's movements. That ought to save us a lot of time once we've also pinpointed things with that detector of yours.'

'Good. Got the fellow surrounded, in fact. Only point now is whether he'll bite or not.'

'Supposing,' Brice said slowly, 'he doesn't?'

'In that case we're not terribly worse off, even though we shall have to go a longer way around. If Cole doesn't bite, we shall at least have proof that he's the man we want.'

Hargraves frowned. 'I don't follow your reasoning.'

'Isn't it obvious that, if Cole doesn't bite, somebody must have let him know that this stunt is a fake? Now there isn't anybody who could have let him know except maybe Judith Mackinley. So if he doesn't accept our offer we know positively that he's the man we want because he's deliberately side-stepped . . . Incidentally, do you know if Judith has told him anything?'

'No idea,' Hargraves said.

Garson grunted something, but before he could comment, Burton, the head cashier, came into the office. He was as impeccably dressed as usual, but his expression was vaguely startled.

'The — er — consignment has arrived, gentlemen,' he announced. 'The vans just drew up outside the bank. Do you wish to witness matters?'

'Not particularly,' Hargraves said. 'It will be plain routine. We'd better get down to the vault and see what happens there.'

'Whatever you wish,' Burton assented. 'If you will come with me . . . '

He left the office and piloted the three men through the back regions of the bank to the underground depths where lay the vault. The massive time-lock door was open and, beyond, a solitary electric light gleamed.

'Splendid!' Garson said, walking into

the strongroom proper and setting down his detector case. 'Now maybe we'll get some action.'

Burton departed to supervise the exterior proceedings, and before long the first men arrived with the heavy wooden boxes, labeled and looking deceptively like the real thing. They were placed in the same position as the real consignment had been, and within an hour every box was duly stacked and in place. It was only then that Judith Mackinley put in an appearance, looking at the dummy gold boxes in faint amusement.

'All correct, gentlemen?' she asked, Burton standing behind her.

'Entirely so,' Hargraves assented. 'All we do now is wait for something to happen.'

'Nothing I can do?' Judith offered, but Sawley Garson shook his head.

'Nothing at all. Just carry on with normal business and leave us to handle the rest.'

The girl nodded, motioned to Burton, and they departed. The vast door was almost closed — then the three men within the vault looked at each other.

'All happy and cosy,' Carson said, swinging open the lid of his mahogany box. 'And this baby all primed up.'

'Better get some chairs.' Hargraves said to Brice. 'We can't stand up all the time. This may take hours.'

It was close on 4 in the morning when Hargraves found himself suddenly being shaken into wakefulness. He opened his eyes blearily to behold Garson looking at him disappointedly.

'I'm afraid it's no use, Hargraves. Nothing's happened. We'd better be packing it up.'

Hargraves yawned and then got to his feet stiffly. Brice also rose beside him, stretching wearily.

'Evidently Cole's wise to us,' Hargraves said grimly. 'All right — that makes it more or less certain that he's our man. I shall have to think up a reasonable excuse for arresting him — then we can start questioning him.'

'No,' Garson said quietly, shaking his head. 'Positively no!'

'Why not?' Hargraves was impatient

with the futility of everything. 'We've failed by so-called scientific methods. Isn't it about time we use orthodox procedure?'

'And how far would you get? Nowhere! If you arrest him, Cole will never say anything, and you can't do anything to nail him without proof. All you can do this time is accept defeat with as good grace as possible. We haven't finished yet.'

'Glad to hear it,' Hargraves growled, tugging open the vast door. 'Let's get out into the fresh air.'

They made their way upstairs into the tiled hall. Hargraves looked morosely at the dark grilles above the counters, then he seemed to suddenly bethink himself.

'Better ring back the Yard and see if there are any messages,' he said, and crossed over to the public telephone on the right of the entrance way. The others moved toward him and then stood waiting. They could not help but hear his own remarks, and their attention became gradually fixed.

'Grantham's, you say? Uh-huh — What! Everything? The night watchman is okay — Eh? He saw this happen — Yes, yes. All right, we'll look into it right away.'

Hargraves rang off and turned an amazed face.

'What's happened?' Garson asked, surprised.

'Things have happened tonight while I've been away. A call has come through from the Grantham Bank. They had their own consignment of gold yesterday — about £500,000 — and the lot has gone! What's more, the night watchman heard queer sounds and investigated. He got the strong-room open — not a time-lock device like this — and went in just in time to see the last gold ingots vanish.' Hargraves took a deep breath. 'They weren't taken away. They just melted into thin air!'

10

For a time there was complete silence in the Mackinley Bank, then suddenly Sawley Garson broke it by laughing heartily.

'What's so funny?' Hargraves demanded angrily.

'Sorry,' Garson apologized, steadying. 'But you'll have to admit that friend Cole is a wise merchant and no mistake. He knows we've been concentrated on this place, sweating blood for the least clue — and what does he do? He robs somewhere else while our attention is elsewhere. I've got to admire the man!'

'I don't see anything to admire in a criminal business like this! He's taken half a million in gold — That isn't funny!'

They let themselves out of the bank and securely locked the door. Then, each in their separate cars, they drove the three miles across the quiet city to Grantham's Bank, to find squad cars already lined up.

Hargraves was immediately admitted to one of the private offices where a colleague of his, Superintendent Meadows, was already in the midst of routine inquiry. In a corner sat a solitary old man, very much bemused — apparently the watchman.

'Evening, sir.' The super saluted and looked rather surprised. 'I was given to understand you were out on a job — '

'I was, but I got news of this,' Hargraves answered. 'The two things may be inter-related. What are the facts?'

'Pretty puzzling ones, sir. This bank had a consignment of gold today — about £500,000 worth. Hearing queer noises from the strongroom around about 3 this morning, the watchman investigated and — '

'Found the gold gone. Yes, I know that much.' Hargraves looked at the watchman. 'You the watchman, sir?'

'Aye, I am.' The old man rose slowly from his chair. 'I'm an old man, sir — a pensioner — but I'd be prepared to swear there ain't nothing wrong with me eyes, not as far as seeing things is concerned.

Yet I saw things tonight! Weird things!'

'Such as?' Hargraves asked testily, tired with his all-night vigil.

'I just got the strong-room door open when I saw three yellow ingots all glowing with light. I switched on the ordinary electric light and rushed forward, but it was too late. The ingots sort of melted. They weren't there any more. I searched the place where they'd been, but there wasn't a sign.'

The superintendent gave a glance that suggested the watchman had been drinking, but Hargraves' expression did not change.

'I credit it, anyway,' Garson said, clapping the old man on the shoulder. 'And I'm glad at last to find somebody who's seen the actual method of stealing the stuff . . . Don't mind me taking over for a moment, Hargraves?'

'Not at all.'

'Now . . . ' Garson hunched forward intently. 'You say these remaining ingots were glowing? Be absolutely precise about it. Did they glitter? Was it a hazy uncertain sort of shine, or what?'

119

'Sort of hazy, with the ingots in the midst of the haze.'

'When you rushed forward to look into things were you aware of any tingling sensation, such as you might get before an ordinary electric radiator when it has been switched on but the element has not had a chance to heat up to the red?'

'There was something like that, sir, yes. Sort of hot feeling on my face and the backs of my hands.'

'Uh-huh . . . Now to something else. What was the noise which first attracted you to the strong-room?'

'There was a sort of humming sound, sir — a very thin, high-pitched note it was. I can't hardly describe it.'

Garson smiled tautly to himself. 'Thanks. I think you've told me all I need to know. Carry on, Hargraves.'

'Seems to me,' Hargraves said, 'there's nothing much to carry on with. You've taken all the relevant particulars, superintendent?'

'Yes, sir — even though I don't quite know what to make of them.'

'All right. Let me have them and I'll

take the business over. This is simply a ramification of the case we're working on at Mackinley's Bank.'

'I understand, sir.'

Hargraves gave Garson a look. 'Anything more, or shall we get back home?'

'This is all I want,' Garson said, making a note or two in his pocketbook. 'Otherwise, we can carry on.'

Hargraves jerked his head to Brice and they hurried out of the building with Garson behind them. At the doors of their respective cars they paused in the first dim light of approaching dawn.

'Well, where do we go from here?' Hargraves asked gruffly.

Garson grinned. 'Home — to catch up on some sleep.'

'I didn't mean that: I meant in regard to the case. Have we merely added another burden, or managed to solve something? I just don't know where I am.'

'We've added this much — Cole knows far more about science than I gave him credit for. Changing metals is smart enough — though quite simple when you have the catalyst — but reducing those metals to atomic form over a distance and then transferring them to some other place is sheer genius ... I've a lot of research to do before I even begin to figure out what our criminal friend has done.'

'Transferring — over a distance?' Hargraves rubbed his face with a tired movement. 'How do you mean?'

'Simply this. The watchman felt a tingling sensation — and before that he heard a sound similar to a high-pitched buzz-saw. Both those conditions are indicative of atomic change — a new patterning of atomic interstices.'

'Oh!' Hargraves shifted uncomfortably as he grasped the car door handle. 'Frankly, I don't understand you. To get down to more earthly matters. What do I do about Cole now he's so neatly fooled us?'

'There's still nothing you can do in the way of a direct accusation against Cole; so you'd better wait until you hear from me. Our one bright hope is that Cole will rob other banks.'

'You call that a bright hope?' Hargraves exclaimed.

'I'd call it our only hope. We shall have to arrange it so that every bank of importance has a detector with a stop-watch action placed in its strong vault: that way one or other of them will point the direction of the theft. It's going to cost a good deal — and it will take some time because I can't trust anybody to make the detectors except myself.' Garson thought for a moment and then nodded. 'Yes — better leave it to me. I'll give you a ring when I've something doped out.'

11

Nine o'clock found Hargraves and Brice both back in the office, cleanly shaved but red-eyed from a sleepless night. Hargraves made it his first duty to phone Judith Mackinley and tell her of the night's failure.

'Oh, too bad!' came the girl's commiserating voice over the wire. 'We pinned such hopes to that move, too. What do you propose to do next, inspector? My directors will want to know.'

'I'm not sure,' Hargraves answered guardedly. 'As a matter of fact, Miss Mackinley, I'd like a serious talk with you on the subject. Would you make it convenient to call upon me on your way to the bank this morning?'

'Certainly, but how can I possibly help?'

'We'll see,' Hargraves answered vaguely, and put the phone down.

In about half an hour Judith arrived.

She smiled seriously as the inspector greeted her and settled in the chair he pushed forward.

'I am going to be blunt about this, Miss Mackinley,' he said calmly. 'Why did you think it necessary to tell Mr. Cole that the bank was baited for a second robbery?'

Judith remained silent, her brown eyes staring. Plainly she was surprised — and not a little hurt.

'I didn't see any reason why I shouldn't. After all, he's my fiancé.'

'Then you did tell him? I wasn't sure of it, but thanks for the corroboration.'

'Inspector, I don't like your attitude, and I particularly resent your line of action against me. It is your job to find the thieves, not take me to task for things I happen to say to my fiancé.'

Hargraves thumped a fist on the desk. 'Listen to me, Miss Mackinley. Because you told your fiancé what the police were doing there was no robbery at your bank last night. Instead, another bank — Grantham's to be precise — was robbed of £500,000 in gold in precisely the same manner as yours. If you'd kept quiet it would never have happened and by now we'd have almost finished the case!'

'But how could saying just a few words to Jeff — '

'Unofficially,' Hargraves interrupted, 'Jeffrey Cole is the man we're after. You asked me yesterday if I considered him guilty and I avoided answering. Now I'm telling you: we have every proof we want, but we can't get at him. I'm taking a risk in telling you this, but if I don't say something, we'll never get anywhere.'

Judith said slowly: 'You mean to tell me that Jeff robbed my father's bank?'

'And Grantham's. There may even be other charges.'

'Other charges? What other charges?'

'I'm not at liberty to say . . . Dropping my role as policeman for a moment, Miss Mackinley, let me warn you that in associating with Cole you're playing with fire.'

'That's a matter of opinion!' Judith's face was strained.

Hargrave shrugged. 'Very well; I'm just giving you the hint, that's all. If you'd help us and transfer your affections from

Cole we could really make headway. Or is that too much to ask?'

'Far too much!' Judith turned to the door. 'I'm sorry, inspector, but whatever opinions you may have about Jeff Cole, I'd prefer definite proof before I believe.' Judith paused with the door half open.

'As a matter of interest, may I inquire what you propose doing next?'

'You will be hearing from me,' Hargraves answered gravely: and with that the girl went out with as much dignity she could muster.

Immediately she had left the inspector's office however, a deeply troubled expression came to her face. It remained with her as she continued, and presently completed, her journey to the bank.

In her private office she attended to routine matters for a while, then gave herself up to serious thought. Finally she reached to the telephone and dialed a number on the private line.

The brisk voice of Jeff Cole answered her.

'Jeff, where are you having lunch

today?' Judith's voice was quiet and serious.

'Where? My usual place. I go to a small café near here. Why, what's the matter? You don't sound too good.'

'I'm all right, but I'd like a talk with you. You know, just feeling lonely, with one thing and another. The funeral tomorrow, and so forth . . . '

'Of course — I understand. I'll pick you up at 10 past 12 and we'll have lunch at Debney's. How's that?'

'Fine,' Judith murmured. 'Fine! See you then.'

She rang off and then pressed the button for the office girl. In a moment this cheerful young teenager presented herself.

'Yes, Miss Mackinley?'

'Betty, there's something I want you to do for me — what you might call a queer job. Here's some money. Go out and buy every morning paper you can think of and bring them here.'

Betty nodded and departed, a very surprised girl.

Judith sat back in her chair, reflecting,

then after a moment she put in another call on the private line — this time to Chief Inspector Hargraves.

'Oh, yes, Miss Mackinley?' He waited expectantly.

'I've been thinking over what you said, chief inspector. Perhaps I was a little rude — and I want to apologize.'

'No need for that, Miss Mackinley. I realize it must have been a shock to you, particularly as you are — or were — so fond of Mr. Cole. However, facts speak for themselves and I told you the truth.'

'I've decided to do something,' Judith continued. 'I am in the position now that I neither believe nor disbelieve you. If I can satisfy myself one way or the other, then I'll know how to act. I'm going to do that this lunch time.'

'I'm glad to hear it.'

'You can help me, in a roundabout way. You mentioned Grantham's Bank had been robbed last night. Is that information going to be published in the newspapers, or will it be hushed up?'

'I left no instructions to hush it up, and

Sir Robert Shepley, governor of the bank, to whom I've been speaking on the phone, hasn't said anything about suppressing the news, so presumably the information will be in the papers. Tonight, of course. I don't suppose anything has leaked into the morning dailies unless some reporter has queried the information-room at the Yard here — as they often do for news items during the night.'

'Thanks,' Judith said. 'That's all I wanted to know.'

With that she rang off and waited with some impatience for the return of Betty with the newspapers.

It was nearly 45 minutes before the girl returned, laden with as many newspapers as she could hold.

'They're all there, every one.' she announced proudly. 'I never thought there were so many dailies on the market . . . And here's the change.'

'Keep it.' Judith smiled. 'You've done a good job.'

Well satisfied with herself, Betty went out, and Judith took the first newspaper from the stack and studied it carefully page by page.

She kept rigidly at the job — except when she had bank matters to attend to — until 12 o'clock, by which time she had got to the last paper. This done, she picked up the whole pile, put them in the bottom drawer of the filing cabinet and closed it.

Then she made her preparations for the arrival of Jeff Cole. Serious-faced, she was at the close of repairing her make-up when Jeff arrived. He was smiling, as usual, but his grey eyes seemed unusually alert, as though he sensed something queer in the atmosphere but could not pin it down.

'Hello, Jeff!' Judith smiled as he kissed her. 'I'm all ready.'

He nodded but did not say anything. They went outside to his car and within 10 minutes were at their usual table in Denby's.

A visit during lunch hour was a new one to Alberti, but he took it in his stride, even managing to seat them at their usual secluded table.

'Something.' Jeff said, when the order had been taken, 'has happened.'

'Has it?' Judith asked mechanically. 'In what way?'

'This sudden decision to need me to talk to is rather odd, is it not?' Jeff asked, as the luncheon was served and the waiter retreated. 'I've always thought of you as so resourceful, so entirely capable of dealing with whatever comes along.'

'I am — usually. This morning, though, I woke up feeling very depressed, and it hasn't worn off either. I thought I might get over it by talking to you.'

Jeff grinned cynically. 'Thanks for the compliment. I never thought I was such a ray of sunshine.'

'I suppose it's the cumulative effect of everything.' Judith continued moodily, toying with her meal indifferently. 'The bank robbery, the death of father, then the failure of the police to get any result last night — '

'They muffed it, then?' Jeff asked. 'That's a pity.'

'Chief Inspector Hargraves can't understand it,' Judith sighed. 'He laid his plans so carefully — yet they misfired. He's even more annoyed because another bank was robbed in the same queer fashion while he was doing sentry duty over ours.'

'And what,' Jeff asked sardonically, 'is the master-mind going to do now?'

'I've no idea. He says wait for his telephone call when he'll let me know the next move in the game.'

'Which is another way of saying he was beaten last night and doesn't know what to do next. That's a nice prospect for public safety!'

'He'll think of something,' Judith said. 'For my own part I hope it's soon. 'There was a letter this morning from Europe concerning the theft from our place, and unless the gold is replaced pretty quickly there'll be trouble . . . On top of that, several of our clients — worthwhile ones, too — have done exactly what dad was afraid they'd do — withdrawn their accounts and taken them elsewhere.'

'To Grantham's, probably,' Jeff grinned. 'Only to find out that things are as bad there. It makes you think.'

Judith was silent, looking at her plate. Then she changed the subject.

'I'm glad you could come to lunch with me, Jeff. I feel a whole lot better for talking to you.'

'Glad to hear it . . . Anything special you want to do tonight or are you waiting until after the funeral tomorrow?'

'Leave it, and I'll phone you,' Judith suggested. 'I haven't quite made up my mind yet.'

Jeff nodded and thereafter, thanks to careful steering on Judith's part, conversation drifted into the commonplace. They parted at Debney's doorway toward 1 o'clock, Judith declining to be driven back to the bank.

'But why not?' Jeff asked in surprise.

'I've a little shopping to do first,' Judith explained. 'I might as well walk.'

'Okay,' Jeff sighed, 'Have it your way . . . I'll wait for your phone call then.'

He switched on the ignition and, waving after him, Judith watched his car slowly merge into the incessant stream of traffic.

As her hand lowered her expression

slowly changed; then she turned and bent her footsteps in the direction of Scotland Yard.

Her original intention had been to leave a message for Chief Inspector Hargraves — whom she had expected to be at lunch — to contact her at the bank.

Rather to her surprise, Hargraves was in his office, and on learning of the girl's presence in the reception area, he gave instructions for her to be shown to his office immediately.

'Have a seat,' he invited, pushing some sandwiches to one side of his desk.

He smiled as the girl seated herself. 'I rather thought you might call or phone after having lunch with Cole: hence my frugal lunch here. Well — anything to tell me?'

'Just one thing.' Judith answered deliberately. 'I'm going to fight on your side now. Jeff let something slip which satisfies me you must be right in your suspicions.'

Hargraves gave her a keen look — and Brice, munching sandwiches in his own corner of the office, looked up expectantly.

'What was this something? Hargraves inquired.

'I told you this morning on the phone that I had a plan — and I put it to work. Before I went to lunch with Jeff I got a copy of every daily newspaper — every one, mind you — and looked through them. Not one of them mentioned the robbery at Grantham's Bank last night.'

'Not surprising. They'd hardly have time to get the information.'

'True, but I wanted to make sure. Anyhow, at lunch I steered the conversation to mentioning that another bank had been robbed — but I didn't say which.'

'Uh-huh. And then?'

'I was trying to think what to say next and I mentioned that one or two good customers at our own bank had withdrawn their accounts. Jeff surprised me by saying they probably put them in Grantham's Bank, only to find there was a robbery there, too. Words to that effect, anyhow — '

'Did he actually say 'Grantham's

Bank'?' Hargraves asked sharply.

'Yes — he did.' Judith tightened her lips. 'That's the whole point: I'd never mentioned the name — deliberately — so how did he know *which* bank it was that had been robbed?'

'You know the answer to that,' Hargraves said gravely.

'I do now,' Judith said, low-voiced. 'I only wish I'd listened to my poor father.'

'One with romantic inclinations rarely sees straight,' Hargraves shrugged. 'However, I'm glad you have the picture in its right perspective before taking an irreparable step. I gather you are now prepared to work with us?'

'In any way I can,' Judith assented frankly.

'Good . . . ' Hargraves pondered a while. 'You may be our most useful ally, Miss Mackinley. It is not uncommon for the police to use their wives and sweethearts and sisters if they need a feminine decoy to gather information, but Cole is not the kind of man to fall for anything like that. On the other hand, he will certainly fall for anything *you* like to spin — providing, and always providing

— you never let him guess the truth. If he does, the result might be tragic.'

'Tragic?' Judith took a tighter grip of her handbag.

'Yes. I'm not going to mince matters, Miss Mackinley. You suspected that your father was murdered. I am also pretty sure of it, and everything points to Cole as the killer.'

Judith gave a start. 'Jeff killed my father? But how — ?'

'The exact method used is still being worked out. If he would kill your father, do you think he would hesitate to kill you? Not for a moment — especially if he discovered you were tricking him. There you have the extent of the potential danger. You still want to go on? I shan't blame you if you decline.'

'No! More so than ever since you believe he killed my father.'

'Very well . . . We have an expert working on this matter, but you can perhaps shorten the road by finding out one very vital piece of information. Discover, by any means you think fit, where Cole has his laboratory.'

Judith frowned. 'Laboratory?' What should he need a laboratory for?'

'To house the scientific apparatus with which he robbed your bank and Grantham's. The robbery was a scientific one, based on electronics. That much we learned from our expert. Until we find that laboratory we're hamstrung. It can be done perhaps with detectors, but that will take time — and again it relies on the fact of Cole making a move, which he might not. If you can find out something, so much the better.'

Judith rose to her feet and gave a somewhat nervous smile. 'I wish I'd seen through Jeff earlier.'

'For myself,' Hargraves said, rising and putting a hand on her arm, 'I dislike sending you into battle in this fashion. That's why I'm making it entirely voluntary. But this robbery is so utterly unusual that we must use unusual means to combat it. There is also the danger that matters will get worse. I don't think Cole will rest content with his present achievements.'

'Neither do I, knowing him as I do.'

12

Hargraves looked up as his office door opened, and Sergeant Brice returned after escorting Judith out of the building. Brice was looking distinctly troubled.

'Why not say it, Harry?' Hargraves asked. 'You think I was out of order asking Miss Mackinley to help us, don't you?'

Brice hesitated before replying.

'Of course not, sir,' he said loyally. 'As you yourself said, we sometimes have to involve members of the public, when it's the only way we can get results. And she did volunteer . . . '

'Then why the long face?'

'Frankly, sir, I'm worried about her safety. Naturally, we'll detail some officers to keep an eye on Cole, but he's such a cunning and ruthless devil that I can't help but think — ' He broke off as his superior's telephone suddenly rang.

Hargraves whipped up the instrument.

'Chief Inspector Hargraves here.'

He listened for a few moments, then said: 'Right! I'll come immediately.'

Hargraves replaced the phone on its cradle and glanced at Brice.

'Get the car, Harry. That was Sawley Garson, ringing from his home. There's been a development he wants us to see.'

★　★　★

It was by no means the first time Chief Inspector Hargraves had found himself summoned somewhat authoritatively to Sawley Garson's home — and he knew that it was a summons he ignored at his peril. So he promptly went, taking Sergeant Brice with him.

As usual, the indefatigable scientist was in his laboratory, apparently not in the least listless after his sleepless, fruitless night.

'Before you tell me why you've sent for me,' Hargraves said, 'there's been a development at our end.' And he outlined what had taken place at his meeting with Judith.

'No more than I expected,' Garson grunted, as Hargraves finished his account of his conversation with the girl. 'That Cole has been confirmed as the guilty party, I mean. As for Miss Mackinley, that girl has courage, and it's up to us to see that her courage is rewarded.' He turned abruptly, and added over his shoulder:

'Follow me: 'I've something to show you. I think you'll be interested.'

He led the way across the laboratory to an affair resembling a big oblong box. On the front of it was an ebonite panel together with all manner of switches and dials. The whole thing was apparently plugged in to a powerful generator in one corner.

'What is it?' Hargraves asked, after a careful study.

'Your insurance against the fact that there will be no more thefts — at least not in this country, and that is what we are principally concerned with.'

Hargraves eyes lighted. 'Good! But what is it?'

'Simply an interrupting wavelength,

which will offset all the efforts of our friend Cole when he uses his apparatus. It has a range of something like 200 miles, which is all we need for a country of our size. Briefly, it sets up a violent interference which will cancel out the wavelength which Cole is using.'

'But you don't know what he is using!' Brice objected, and Garson made an impatient gesture.

'Give me time! Here are the facts — I learned a good deal from our watchman friend at Grantham's Bank. He spoke of the gold disappearing into a mist for one thing, which in itself points undeniably to a wavelength able to both transmute stuff into atomic form and also withdraw the 'atomic parcel' when it has formed. Therefore, the wavelength Cole is using has a dual quality. It is both transmutative and magnetic. See?'

'I'm trying to,' Hargraves said, screwing up his eyes.

'Look at it this way. I'll explain to you what Cole is doing. He is able, from a distance, to reduce gold — or any other metal as well, I suppose — to its atomic components. In doing that there is, of course, a tremendous shrinkage until actual atomic size is reached, in which state the original object is invisible to the eye. It has lost its expanded, material form and becomes simply a parcel of atomic forces, if you will. To put it more plainly: imagine a balloon blown up to enormous size. That represents the normal gold. Along comes something that lets the air out of the balloon. It reduces, and for the sake of our picture, let's say it reduces to invisibility. Right! That is the gold in its atomic, invisible form. Once that is done a magnetic wave comes into it; which draws the atomic parcel — inconceivably tiny — back to the starting point. And by starting point I mean the machine which is causing the reduction.'

'Definitely the man's a genius,' Hargraves said, with a grudging admiration.

'No doubt of that, but unfortunately he isn't using his genius in the right way. By a simple adjustment of his machinery he should be able to make anything in the atomic scale vanish at will — or be transmutated. That is why he is such a menace, or rather would have been except for my interference field. Add to this knowledge the fact that he also has the secret of a catalyser for changing elements and we begin to get the full stature of the man's scientific accomplishments.'

'You'd wonder that a man with such scientific knowledge doesn't share it with the world,' Hargraves said disgustedly.

'When he has the power to steal almost anything he wants? When he can, unfortunately, kill as he chooses?' Garson shook his head. 'I'm afraid the temptation of infinite power has proved too strong for Cole.'

'You said something about killing as he chooses,' Hargraves reflected. 'Do you suppose Joseph Mackinley was one of his victims?'

'It could be done,' Garson mused. 'Definitely it could . . . '

Garson was silent, his quick mind pursuing this new line of interest. Then presently he nodded to himself.

'Using very fine limits it could be done, but care would have to be exercised to be sure nobody but Mackinley himself got in the way of the beam. Hmm. I don't see how one could do it at a distance. Far too many people would be in the way of the beam, and they'd all suffer. This was exclusive concentration.'

Hargraves and Brice both waited, struggling to keep up with the scientist's half-muttered asides.

'First, the technical side,' Garson said, arousing himself to speak clearly. 'If the apparatus were adjusted to fine limits and used as an extremely narrow beam, it could produce heart failure by contraction of the heart to the point where it stopped beating. A moment's work with the beam in reverse could restore the heart to normal size, but it wouldn't beat again. Result to the medical man — heart failure. Simple.'

'Simple, but horrifying.' Hargraves said with a half shiver. 'I take it, then, that this apparatus can enlarge or contract any object at will?'

'Of course. I thought I'd made that clear. Contraction is the main object, of course — but in a case like Mackinley's I imagine enlargement back to normal would be needed. You see, even in the case of this gold it has to be brought back to normal in order that the catalytic process can be applied to change its nature.'

'Mmmm,' Hargraves responded, vaguely. 'But look here — about Mackinley. If it couldn't be done at a distance, how do you think it might be done?'

Garson shrugged. 'Perhaps by a small portable edition of the big apparatus. It wouldn't have to be large for a job like that. Everything could be incorporated in a smallish box. But there's the question of power — ' Garson snapped his fingers. 'The engine of a car! If it had a generator of sufficient strength it could supply the apparatus.'

Hargraves did not say anything. He had his brows down in fierce concentration.

'An ordinary car generator wouldn't do?' he questioned

'I don't think so, not powerful enough. It would need an auxiliary one specially fitted.'

'And with Cole owning a garage that

would be an easy job,' Brice put in. 'That what you're thinking, sir?'

'Yes. Cole has a powerful racing car: I've seen it.'

'I've one or two things I'd like to ask about this scientific set-up,' Brice said. 'You don't mind, sir?'

'Go ahead.'

'When the gold is reduced to such smallness as to be merely atomic and invisible, how can it go through walls and so forth back to the starting point?'

'Because, my friends, it is less resistant than the walls,' Garson shrugged. 'Material things are not really solid, remember: they only appear so to the eye. These reduced packets of atomic gold simply slide through the spaces in matter, as easily as water passes through a colander.'

Brice scratched the back of his head and nodded, none too vigorously, either.

'There's another point,' he went on doggedly. Regarding this interference machine of yours — Is it switched on now?'

'It is.'

'Well, won't it create a tremendous lot

of interference with television and radio reception? Cole's does, along the track of the beam, so how about yours?'

'Insufficient power for that,' Garson answered. 'All I do is very slightly upset Cole's beam, which will make it impossible for him to pinpoint any specific place. It's no more than a whisper of interference, but it's enough to upset the delicate balance, I believe. We'll soon know when Cole decides to rob somewhere else.'

'And he'll know you are interfering with his beam?' Brice asked.

'I don't see how he *can* know. He might guess, but he will not be able to trace the course of the upset. In the meantime,' Garson continued, looking at Hargraves, 'we'll get those small detectors in every bank of importance, and they will tell us plenty.'

'How will they?' Hargraves questioned. 'If you have offset his beam, so to speak, it won't register on the detectors, will it?'

'It will register all right — long enough to affect a stop-action detector, but Cole won't be able to maintain a steady position long enough to steal anything. I've thought all that out.'

'And, candidly, thank heaven you have,' Hargraves sighed. He glanced at Brice.

'It's only just gone 2 o'clock. I think we should visit the Mackinley residence and have a good look around for any signs of Cole's car having been there. Some of the neighbors might have seen something too.'

'What about my detectors?' Garson asked. 'You're going to back my scheme, of course?'

'Definitely!' Hargraves affirmed. 'If you'll allow me to use your phone before we leave, I'll get the wheels in motion.'

13

After an afternoon varying between spells of hard work and silent reflection on Jefferson Cole, Judith prepared herself for her meeting with him that evening — which appointment she had made by phone on returning from Hargraves' office.

She had full awareness of what she was attempting, but this did not in any way dampen her ardor. In particular she remembered how her father had warned her against Cole, and in particular how he had died. That alone was sufficient to make her want to get at the truth.

She returned home long enough to freshen up, and then set out for Debney's restaurant, walking it instead of using her car.

She wanted the chance to weigh things up quietly to herself until the very last moment — in which frame of mind she finally entered Debney's and found the inevitable Alberti hovering before her.

It was not very long before she caught sight of Jeff, in his customary neat lounge suit, making his way toward her. Reaching the table, he gave her a broad smile.

'Good! Best news I've had for weeks — that you'd decided to cock a snoot at convention and dine with me.' He seated himself. 'Makes it like old times.'

'Cock a snoot at convention?' Judith repeated. 'What do you mean by that?'

'I mean that you have decided that I am more important than the rules — the rules of staying put until after your dad's funeral.'

'Oh — I see.' Judith gave a little shrug. 'I just got to thinking that one can't live with the dead, so there it is.'

Silence. And for some reason Judith found it unbearable. She could sense Jeff's cold grey eyes boring at her; yet his next remark was quite commonplace.

'Any ideas for this evening? Show or anything?'

Judith purposely demurred. 'I don't think it had better be a show. I'm pretty well known, and if anybody happened to see me they'd think me the last word in callousness in view of what's happening tomorrow. How about a ride around for a change?'

'All right with me — ' Jeff was silent as the waiter returned with the meal. Then: 'Anywhere particular in mind?'

'No — just anywhere where we can talk. After all, seeing that we are to be married soon, we don't seem to have much chance to exchange confidences.'

'Are there some?' Jeff asked dryly.

'For one thing, I haven't seen these garage extensions you keep talking about. Any reason why I can't?'

'No reason at all. It's hardly a top secret.'

Judith started her meal, thinking what she ought to say next. She could hardly come straight to the point, so what she had said so far seemed the next best thing.

'Seen Chief Inspector Hargraves today?' Jeff asked suddenly, and with a start Judith looked up. She found Jeff was smiling, apparently quite pleasantly.

'Well — yes, I have. About the failure

last night to catch the thief at the bank.'

'While he was busy at your bank, over at Grantham's Bank instead, you mean?' The grey eyes became fixed and the smile faded.

'I remembered, this afternoon, that I made a mistake in mentioning Grantham's Bank by name,' Jeff added slowly. 'Silly of me, wasn't it?'

Judith went on with her meal but her heart was thudding violently. She kept telling herself there was nothing to be afraid of. 'Very,' Judith replied shortly, raising her eyes. 'Of all the ridiculous things to say!'

'Ridiculous? I wonder!' Jeff meditated for a moment. 'It just goes to show how careful one must be. One chance statement — and you lose a friend — completely.' His tone changed.

'You being a quite intelligent girl with her head screwed on the right way, naturally found it necessary to tell Chief Inspector Hargraves of what I had said?'

'Not at all. I — '

'Don't lie, Judith! I know you too well!' Jeff's voice was still quiet, but it was as hard as steel. Judith looked up again to meet the icy grayness in his eyes.

'All right, I did tell Chief Inspector Hargraves,' she said deliberately. Abruptly Judith flung down her napkin and rose to her feet.

'Since matters have come to a head, I don't think I've anything more to say to you — or you to me.'

'Speak for yourself,' Jeff answered. 'And don't imagine you're going anywhere because you're not! Sit down!'

Judith hesitated; then she slowly looked down at Jeff's right hand.

It was half covered by a napkin, and projecting from under the whiteness was a dark blue muzzle of unusual thinness.

'It's a nitric acid jet,' Jeff explained calmly. 'It won't kill but it will certainly maim — permanently. I call it a persuader ... Better sit down, hadn't you?'

There was nothing Judith could do. She sat — staring fixedly.

'It's a pity things had to take this turn between us,' Jeff resumed. 'I had great hopes of making you my wife — but that

can never be now, of course. Unless . . . '
He paused and smiled twistedly.

'Unless . . . unless you care to play the game my way. I can — and will — give you the earth in time.'

Judith hesitated, trying to make up her mind whether she ought to play along with Jeff in order to find out the information she wished to know — but she prolonged her hesitation too far.

'All right,' Jeff said suddenly. 'So you won't play the game my way. That's a pity! Er — you suggested a ride around this evening, didn't you?'

'How can you even think of such a thing the way things are now?' Judith whispered huskily.

'Why shouldn't I? Maybe I'll be able to change your mind about a lot of things . . . ' Jeff hardened his tone.

'Now listen to me, Judy, and face facts! We're going to leave here together as though nothing is different between us — but if you make any sign, any false move whatsoever, I'll be right behind you. You'll get a taste of a medicine you won't like, even if I have to make a dash for it afterwards. Take things sensibly and no harm will come to you. Understand?'

Judith gave a desperate glance about her. There was nobody anywhere near enough to them at whom to direct any kind of appeal for help.

Whilst the restaurant was fairly crowded, her social eminence had secured them her usual isolated table. As ever, Alberti was watching their table from a discreet distance. But he was too far away to have overheard any of her conversation with Jeff.

She shrugged helplessly.

'How can I help but do so?'

'Good!' Smiling coldly, Jeff rose to his feet. He kept one hand in his pocket, the hand containing the acid gun. As he rose, Alberti came hurrying ever.

'I trust there is nothing wrong, Mr. Cole?' he asked anxiously. 'You have not dined so fully as usual.'

'There's nothing wrong with the meal, Alberti — don't think that,' Jeff smiled easily. 'It's just that we have a rather pressing engagement elsewhere, haven't we, dear?'

Judith did not answer. She tried by her facial expression to convey some kind of message to Alberti, but it was plain he did not understand her; then she desisted and relaxed as Jeff looked at her sharply.

Taking her arm, he led her across the crowded restaurant toward the swing doors.

Desperately Judith cudgeled her brain to think of something to save herself, but over every idea that came there hung the perpetual threat of Jeff's acid gun. Perhaps there might be some other and less dangerous way . . .

'After you,' Jeff was saying suddenly — and Judith realized she had come to his powerful racer at the curb. For a brief moment she hesitated, but Jeff stood there relentless.

Quietly she opened the door and slid down into the bucket seat. Jeff snapped the door shut behind her and smiled with his lips alone; then in a moment he had hurried around the car and eased himself into the driving seat.

'Anywhere in particular?' he asked dryly.

'Scotland Yard perhaps?' Judith gave him a bitter look and his grin widened.

He switched on the ignition, put in the first gear, and roared noisily into the midst of the swirling traffic.

'I know you expected the countryside,' Jeff murmured, watching the road in front of him, 'but things have changed somewhat. In view of what's happened I think there's something I ought to show you.'

Judith did not comment. There was not much she could do now beyond waiting, and seize her chance when it came.

Jeff did not make any further observations: he drove in and out of the traffic until eventually he pulled up at a wide, curiously empty stretch for the heart of London — an area indeed left over from a clearance scheme, an area not yet entirely rebuilt into blocks of flats and shops.

Jeff pulled up and pointed. 'See that?'

Judith found herself looking at about the only building in the area — a low-built one-story affair in the modern style. From the outward appearance it looked exactly like a bungalow. Beyond doubt it was new. The paintwork shone brightly in the evening light.

'Well?' she asked, and Jeff grinned.

'I own it. Nobody's aware of the fact except you. Even the man who built it has never seen me. I've used a different name and done everything through an agent. And the machinery inside it has been bought from various firms, so none of them can connect up the whole story. I admit it's cost me plenty, but for the profit I'm going to make, it's worth it.'

Jeff glanced about him for a moment, as if to be sure there was nobody in sight — which apparently there was not — then he drove the car forward, turning it abruptly on to the deserted site where the building stood.

Judith held her breath as Jeff did not slow down in the slightest. She was convinced he was going to drive straight into the wall, and instinctively ducked her head.

There was no crash — such as Judith had expected. At the last moment, as the racer swept forward, the whole side wall of the building shot to one side, and Jeff, obviously accustomed to the set-up from long experience, drove into a tiny garage. The wall — or door — shot back into place and Judith was convinced that the floor slowly sank. She could see the wall sliding past in the headlights.

With difficulty Judith edged herself out in the narrow space and then stood up. Between the wall and the car there was only just room for Jeff and herself to stand.

'Now come this way,' he ordered curtly, and though she had a strong premonition of danger, Judith could do nothing but obey.

Jeff led the way around to the doorway on the opposite wall and pressed his hand against the apparently smooth paintwork. In a moment the door opened and lights came up automatically beyond. He stood aside for Judith to enter.

Slowly she did so. In spite of herself, she could not help but be impressed by the wilderness of machinery and technical equipment.

Her knowledge of such things was, of course, limited, but she easily recognized switchboards, panels, and a couple of generators. There were also several curious devices with screens attached that excited her interest.

Then Jeff came slowly forward, closing the door behind him.

'Interested?' he inquired, a strange note in his voice. 'In case you don't know it, Judith, you're gazing on the machinery which is going to unlock for me the gates of power.'

Quite unexpectedly Jeff made a dive for her. Before she could do a thing he had seized her tightly and whirled her towards a metal cage.

Almost before she realized it, Judith found herself within the cage and the metal-work tightly clamped around her. She struggled frantically but found it impossible to move more than a fraction of an inch.

'Let me out of here!' Judith beat savagely on the metal-work.

Jeff shook his head, smiling coldly.

'No, my dear, I'm sorry. That's just what I don't intend to do. I'm very sorry, but since you've refused to play the game my way, I've got to be rid of you — as I

162

did your father . . . '

'So it *was* you!' Judith cried, tears springing to her eyes. 'The police told me that they suspected as much — '

'Good for them — but without proof, they won't be able to touch me.'

'When I get out of here, I'll soon tell them what you've just admitted.'

Jeff gave a harsh laugh. 'You don't know how funny that is!' Then his tone hardened, became deadly:

'I'm afraid you are going to take a short journey, and there will be no proof of where you went, how you went, or where you have gone to. I'm not going to explain it, either. I doubt if your silly little mind could grasp it.'

With that, Jeff suddenly snapped a switch. Judith screamed as a sensation like a thousand pins and needles flooded through her.

To her anguished eyes came the vision of the laboratory becoming mist-like, wavering crazily . . . and then it was gone . . .

Jeff for his part kept his eyes rigidly on the cage. He smiled as he saw the figure of Judith become wraith-like before his eyes.

When he switched off the apparatus the cage was completely empty.

14

Toward tea-time, Chief Inspector Hargraves and Sergeant Brice returned to their office in Whitehall, neither of them in a particularly cheerful frame of mind.

Hargraves flung his hat on the peg. 'I don't think we ever spent a more fruitless afternoon, Harry.'

'No, sir. Pretty bad show all around. Garson's guess about Cole's car being the answer to a portable weapon may have been correct, but without any proof that Cole's car was parked near the Mackinley residence at the time of his death we're sunk.'

'No tracks, no information from possible observers — nothing. Not even a mark on the stonework outside Mackinley's bedroom.' Hargraves compressed his lips. 'That's one line of inquiry which will have to await verification from Cole himself, when we finally get enough on him to bring him in.'

Brice nodded gloomily. 'Wonder if Judith Mackinley's managed to make a date with Cole as she expected?'

'No idea. Afraid she'll have to take her chance from here on. Our boys are keeping track of Cole anyhow if he attempts anything funny.'

So the time passed. Six o'clock and 7 o'clock came and went.

Brice was just on the point of inquiring whether or not they could wrap it up for the day when a plainclothesman walked into the office. Hargraves glanced up, recognizing him immediately as one of the men detailed to keep watch on Cole's movements

'Well?' Hargraves asked. 'Something to tell me?'

'Thought I'd better make a report, sir. We saw Cole leaving Debney's restaurant with Miss Mackinley. He was using his red racer — and we have its registration. We followed him through the traffic and he turned left at — '

'All right, all right, you're not a guide book.' Hargraves rose to his feet. 'Where did he finish up?'

'Er — that's it, sir. We don't know. He vanished into thin air.'

Hargraves stared. 'He what? That's a fine thing for a qualified man to say! Thin air, indeed!'

'Well, of course it couldn't be that,' the man confessed, 'but the effect looked that way. We were following him into the town center — Embankment Road, to be exact, where there's a big redevelopment site ending in a cul-de-sac. We were delayed for a moment or two by a truck. When we got free we raced into Embankment Road, the only possible way Cole could have gone, but there wasn't a sign of him.'

Hargraves frowned and scratched his chin.

'There's nothing anywhere in the cleared area except a bungalow — new style,' the man added. 'Not even a garage attached to it into which Cole might somehow have slipped. We studied the bungalow but that didn't get us anywhere. It's a complete mystery to us where he went.'

'Embankment Road,' Hargraves repeated, making a note on his scratch pad and then turning to the wall map of London and its environs. 'There's got to be some sort of answer for this — Here, show me exactly where you mean.'

The man nodded and started to find the position on the map, then he paused as the telephone shrilled. Hargraves, nearest to the instrument, whipped it up.

'Yes? Hargraves here . . . ' Then he stood and listened attentively, his expression slowly changing.

'She's all right, you say? Huh? Yes — yes, dazed. No signs of injury? Okay, keep her there if you are quite certain she doesn't need hospital treatment. Oh, she doesn't? Wants to see me right away! Right — I'll be there.'

Hargraves put the phone down and thought for a moment. Brice and the man looked at him inquiringly.

'An extraordinary thing,' he said at length. 'Judith Mackinley has called the police from a place called Balham Road — in the region of Hampstead. Hampstead! Note that! It's some five miles out of the region of Embankment Road. Couple of patrolmen answered her call immediately and found her suffering from shock, but nothing serious. She won't explain herself and only wants to talk to me.'

'You're going to see her?' Brice asked.

'Of course I am, man! Get the car out again!'

Minutes later Sergeant Brice was giving the police car all the speed he could manage in the stream of traffic.

With a screech of brakes he pulled up in front of a stationary police car in Balham Road. A patrolman was standing alongside it.

'The girl all right?' Hargraves asked quickly, alighting from his own vehicle.

'Yes, sir. She's in the car ... ' The patrolman motioned, and at that moment Judith herself scrambled out of the police car and stood up.

She appeared in good shape even though she was a trifle disheveled.

'What happened?' Hargraves grasped her arm. 'Feel able to talk?'

'Surely. I'm okay ... As to what happened, I just don't know. I wanted to tell you that ... that I know where

Jeff's laboratory is.'

The girl hesitated and swayed slightly, a strange look in her eyes. Hargraves caught hold of her anxiously.

'You all right?'

'Not — not as steady as I thought — ' Judith started to say; then quite suddenly she collapsed completely. And it seemed to be something more than a faint, too.

'She's been okay up to now,' the patrolman said in surprise, as he and Hargraves lifted her gently into the car and set her down in the bucket seat. 'Queer thing.'

'Get an ambulance here quickly,' Hargraves said curtly. 'We can't afford to take chances.'

★　★　★

Within 20 minutes Judith had been transported to the nearest hospital and, grimly impatient, Hargraves stalked up and down the reception office awaiting the doctor's opinion.

'If anything serious has happened to that girl I'll never forgive myself,' he told

Brice. 'I asked her to see Cole again, and if that devil has — '

He paused as the doctor came into the office and quietly closed the door.

'Well, doctor?' Hargraves asked. 'How bad is it?'

The doctor hesitated, then:

'Well, the most normal upset about her is one we can get to grips with,' he said. 'Amnesia — produced by violent shock.'

'Amnesia,' Hargraves repeated slowly. 'Which certainly puts us in rather a spot. We were relying on her for some particular information. Anything else wrong with her?'

The doctor gave a queer, half-baffled smile.

'It will interest you to know that the x-ray we gave her reveals the most amazing fact. Every one of her organs that should be on the left of the body are on the right — and vice versa. She looks — as one might look in a mirror, with everything left right, and right to left.'

Hargraves compressed his lips. 'How do you account for this extraordinary business?'

'I don't. It's quite beyond me, and I freely admit it.'

'Would it be possible for us to see her?'

'Certainly — but it won't do you any good.'

In a few moments Hargraves and Brice found themselves in the private room in which the girl was lying.

In silence they looked at her, and the left-to-right effect — which they had not observed before in the excitement of the situation — was now quite noticeable. It was rather like looking at a photograph in which the negative has been reversed before printing.

'Miss Mackinley,' Hargraves said quietly, taking her hand.

She turned her eyes toward him but made no response.

'We can probably do plenty for her in regard to her memory,' the doctor said, when they were in the corridor. 'Modern methods of overcoming amnesia are pretty effective. Whom do I contact to report progress? What about her parents?'

Hargraves smiled grimly. 'Don't you

read the papers, doctor? She's Judith Mackinley — *the* Judith Mackinley, and daughter of Mackinley the banker. It's his funeral tomorrow. All you can do is contact her mother and keep me posted as well.'

'I was not aware that she was of the Mackinley banking family,' the doctor admitted. 'Naturally, this information will have to go into the press, with a good few trimmings.'

'I'd rather it didn't,' Hargraves said. 'There are vital reasons why it shouldn't. Keep everything as dark as possible, and I'll contact Mrs. Mackinley and see that she does likewise. I have a vague suspicion that Judith has been nearly murdered, and it may help us a lot if her potential murderer thinks he got away with it. Understand?'

'Very well. Cases are suppressed, of course, if a request is made. Since you represent the police, your wishes will be entirely respected.'

'Good.' Hargraves gave a nod. 'We'll leave it at that, doctor. We've things to do . . . Come on, Harry.'

'What now, sir?' Brice asked, as they again got into the car.

'We'll try Garson. I'm getting a bit tangled up and I could do with some suggestions.'

Brice nodded and swung the car down the driveway and into the main street.

They reached Sawley Garson's residence within 15 minutes and found him in the midst of building the small radiation detectors.

'And what's the matter now?' he asked, as the two men were shown in to him by the housekeeper.

'Plenty,' Hargraves grunted. 'We got the location of Cole's laboratory within our grasp, and then lost it again — thanks to amnesia.'

'Whose?'

'Judith Mackinley's.' And Hargraves went through the whole sequence of events. By the time he had finished, Garson had his briar out and was dragging at it thoughtfully.

'Most interesting,' he commented. 'Most!'

'How do you account for it?' Hargraves

demanded. 'What do you imagine happened to Judith?'

'I've no need to imagine what happened to her: I know. The switch in her physical arrangement is enough for me. She must have been reduced to her atomic make-up, and in the restoration, things did not come back precisely the same as they started. They got — transplanted, as it were.'

Hargraves looked rather blank. 'You're talking about a woman, Garson — not a chunk of iron.'

'I'm aware of it, but it doesn't signify. Anything organic or inorganic — indeed, anything at all which is material — is atomic in essence. So I repeat, an attempt was made to reduce Judith to her atomic constituents, but something went wrong and she was restored — though not completely. Our ingenious friend Cole was foiled, for the simple reason that my interference circuit was in operation, and Cole was not aware of the fact.'

Hargraves digested Garson's amazing analysis. 'I'm sure you're right, Garson — though I don't pretend to understand one half of it. But there's still another mystery.'

'Tell me about it.'

'One of the boys followed Cole and Judith before all this happened to Judith, and Cole's car mysteriously vanished into thin air,' Hargraves said. 'Obviously it couldn't have done that, so I think we ought to investigate the only likely spot — a bungalow on a clearance area. Embankment Road to be exact. West central region.'

'A bungalow?' Garson raised his eyebrows. 'That doesn't sound much like a laboratory to me.'

'Nor to me, but it's the last place toward which Cole's car was seen heading. In spite of my boys having looked at this bungalow, I think we'd better do something about it ourselves. And if that fails then maybe we can pull a different kind of bait with Judith.'

'Judith? Garson repeated.

'Well, Cole thinks she's dead — and I've taken pains to have all news about her being alive suppressed. If we can use her in some way to bait Cole, perhaps even trick him into a confession — '

'Maybe.' Garson assented. 'Anyhow, it will bear thinking about. I agree with you that it's better to let Cole think she's dead. Right, so we go and appraise this bungalow, do we'? I'm with you.'

★ ★ ★

Hargraves and Garson looked ahead to a deserted area near the end of the cul-de-sac. Indifferent street lighting cast down upon a new-style, unusually long bungalow with a dirt and cinder frontage instead of a front garden.

'Queer looking place,' Garson commented. 'Sure this is the spot?'

'According to the map, it must be,' Hargraves answered. 'Stop the car, Harry. We'll take a closer look.'

Hargraves leading the way, the three men alighted and hurried towards the bungalow.

When Hargraves reached the main window, which presumably belonged to the living-room, he stared at it fixedly — then indicated the neat flower-patterned curtains drawn across.

'From the look of things we're not going to get much change out of this,' he commented. 'And we daren't go in and look for ourselves without a search warrant.'

'You daren't as policemen,' Garson commented. 'But I dare, and there are several reasons why I think I should. For one thing, those aren't curtains you're looking at, man. They're a polaroid design inset into one-way glass. The way they catch the light — and this street light is pretty ghastly anyway — they look exactly like curtains. Now — why one-way glass in a perfectly normal bungalow?'

'One way?' Hargraves repeated. 'Looking which way?'

'Looking from the inside to the out. See . . . ' Garson went forward to draw attention to some point in the glass, then as he touched the wall he jolted back violently, rubbing his arm and swearing.

'Electrified!' he exclaimed, as Brice and Hargraves looked at him in astonishment.

'And pretty strong voltage, too! Fortunately for me I'm pretty resistant to electric shocks in my business, so there's no harm done — but a child playing around here could be killed instantly.'

'So that's it!' Hargraves' face was grim. 'There's no need to electrify an ordinary bungalow.'

Garson patted his pockets industriously and presently brought a small screwdriver to light. Then, as well as he could in the dim light, he went on a tour of investigation until he finally located a point where the electrified wire was in view.

With the screwdriver, and bracing himself for a brief shock, he short-circuited the current by passing it from the bare copper wire, through the screwdriver shaft, thence to earth by means of a gutter earth-pipe. The wire blackened at the point of contact after sparking sharply, and Garson gasped as current rippled through him — then the job was done.

Carefully he tested the length of wiring and found it completely dead.

'Okay,' he said, as Hargraves and Brice watched him. 'It's blown a fuse somewhere and killed the juice. Let's get inside.'

The obvious choice seemed the front door and without any hesitation, Garson smashed the glass and reached inside. The lock was more or less of the usual variety, so to open the front door was no problem. This done, Garson hesitated and looked into the dark void beyond.

'Wait!' Brice exclaimed suddenly. 'There's a torch in the car. I'll get it.'

In a few moments he was back, fanning a bright beam into a perfectly conventional but entirely empty hall. There were no stairs, of course — just the plain boarded floor with the doors of rooms going off on either side.

'Seems normal enough.' Hargraves remarked disappointedly, pushing the door shut as well as he could. 'Certainly doesn't resemble a laboratory in any shape or form.'

Garson did not seem to be listening. Holding the torch, he was looking intently at the floor where it joined the skirting board and wall.

Presently he investigated the other side of the room. Then finally he directed the beam upwards and looked at the ceiling.

'I believe I've got it,' he said slowly. 'Obviously there is a lighting system somewhere in this place — remember the belt I got from electricity outside. The other interesting point is that the wall and floor are a hairbreadth apart from each other. But the ceiling is not . . . What do you make of it, Hargraves?'

Hargraves took the torch and looked for himself. Finally he rubbed his chin pensively.

'I can't think why the floor doesn't quite touch the wall.' he confessed.

'Well, I can,' Garson shrugged. 'We're not on a floor at all: we're on something like the top of a lift cage. Hydraulic system.'

Hargraves blinked and gave a glance at Brice.

'In other words,' Garson continued, 'this bungalow is just a blind on the off chance that somebody should get in — if they ever could by dodging the electric safeguard. What would be found? Just an empty bungalow with nothing suspicious about it. Okay so far?'

'It hangs together,' Hargraves admitted.

'Right. But when Cole uses his laboratory whatever is below can be raised by hydraulic pressure.'

'Very ingenious,' Hargraves agreed, 'but why raise everything to this level?'

'Possibly the intervention of solid earth interferes with the efficiency of Cole's atomic beam. Possibly, too, he finds it hard to get the right direction with earth intervening. Certainly he would do a lot better at surface level. That's probably the reason. And I'm sure I'm right about the set-up. The point is: how does one get at this buried laboratory? There must be a way somehow.'

15

'There doesn't seem to be anything we can find by fishing around inside here,' Hargraves said, after a long silence. 'Should we try outside and see what we can find? There's the vital point that Cole must have done something with his car for it to vanish as it did. But what?'

'A wily devil like Cole would make ample provision,' Garson snapped. 'Come on — see what we can find.'

They went outside together and then began a slow perambulation of the bungalow, studying it as they went.

'We'd better weigh this up,' Garson said finally, as they paused to consider.

'Let us first assume that Cole would guess at the possibility of people looking around this bungalow — of which we have proof by his electrical precaution. He allows for that possibility by making the bungalow proof against anybody approaching it. What I mean is, his secret opening does not reveal itself just because of a group of people, or even one person approaching.'

'Clear as mud,' Hargraves commented sourly. 'What on earth are you talking about?'

'I'm thinking chiefly of a photoelectric cell somewhere. Cole is a scientist and he'd probably use the photoelectric cell idea. Not that it's original. Thousands of quite everyday folk use them in some form or other . . . All right, taking that into consideration it's unlikely that anybody would tour around this bungalow in a car.'

'Highly unlikely,' Hargraves agreed.

'Yet Cole, on the other hand, would always use a car. Now — a photocell beam that would react to the bulk of a car passing across it might easily miss one person or group of persons, depending how it was adjusted. So, since Cole must always use a car when he comes here — or at least it's a reasonable assumption — we will do likewise and see what happens.'

Hargraves nodded and they hurried

over to the police car, still standing where they had left it.

'I'll drive,' Garson said, slipping behind the wheel. 'I want to try this for myself and it would take too long to keep giving instructions.'

He switched on the ignition as Hargraves and Brice settled in the back seat, then they waited interestedly as the car moved forward on to the cindery waste land in front of the bungalow.

Neither of them were really expecting anything to happen, therefore it came as a distinct surprise when something did. As Garson began to tour around the bungalow a portion of its solid wall abruptly rose, revealing a garage-like space.

'Good!' Garson exclaimed, his eyes bright. 'I was right!'

'Well, how far does this get us?' Hargraves asked, looking about him. 'We're still on the ground-floor level with no means of getting below.'

'There can only be one answer to that,' Garson said.

After a brief manoeuvre, Garson

suddenly turned the car about and drove it nose-first into the tiny garage. The moment he had driven to the limit and stopped, headlights ablaze, the 'doorway' or bungalow wall slammed back into place. When that happened the car began to sink gently, foot by foot.

'Counterweight system,' Garson commented, waiting tensely as the walls slid past and apparently upwards. 'Very nicely planned job, even though I say so.'

With a gentle bump, after sinking by its own weight for about 10 feet, the car halted amidst plain walls. But against the farther wall was a door — the one Judith Mackinley had seen. In a matter of moments the three men had reached it.

Experimental pushing against the wall all around the door finally led Garson to the spot that Cole had pressed upon when Judith had been with him. There was a sudden click and the door quietly opened, lights automatically coming up beyond.

'Better wedge the door,' Garson cautioned. 'We don't want to be trapped.'

Brice spent a few moments wedging

the door with a tire lever from the car's emergency tools; then the three men stood on the threshold and surveyed the laboratory before them.

'Magnificent!' Garson murmured, having a better idea than the two policemen of the significance of the machinery. 'Small, but superb. Let's have a look around.'

He moved over to the vacuum-tube apparatus. 'Here, I take it, is the equipment for the transmutation of elements.' He stood still for a moment and then picked up a small yellow block from the bench. 'Gold, as I live and breathe!' he exclaimed.

'Bank gold?' Hargraves questioned, moving forward

'No — just gold. Probably something Cole's been transmutating.' Garson put the block down again thoughtfully and looked at the strange cage affair in which Judith had been trapped before being 'projected' so unsuccessfully.

'Some kind of projection-matrix,' he explained.

Then, turning to Hargraves: 'Can you arrest Cole for owning stuff like this, or prove he owns it?'

Hargraves sighed and relapsed into thought. At length he seemed to make up his mind.

'My guess is that he's used an alias to construct this bungalow. There's only one certain way out of this — to get Cole on the actual premises without having to wait heaven knows how long for him to move of his own accord. We must use a different kind of bait this time — Judith, to be exact.'

'All right,' Garson said. 'But from what I've heard, she's in no shape to do anything, as I suppose you realize.'

'I realize it — but she won't have to do anything. There's still time to contact the press — and here's what I suggest. We'll splash the fact that Judith is in hospital, and we'll say which one, even to which room. But we'll not advertise the fact that she's lost her memory. The gist of the statement will be that this day — that is tomorrow — on the day of her father's funeral — Judith has decided to tell the real facts of his death, and to reveal all she knows about his killer, and the killer's future plans. She will also reveal to the police the attempt that was made on her life, where from, and the means adopted to steal gold from the Mackinley and Grantham banks — in other words, the lot! What do you think Cole will do when he reads about that?'

Brice looked dubious.

'Might he not wonder that she hasn't said something to the police before this? He's smart enough to suspect the whole thing.'

'Smart enough,' Hargraves agreed, as Garson looked at him intently, 'but he'll still be governed by the fact that she hasn't yet spoken and that because of that he must — absolutely must — stop her.'

'And my interference wave will offset things if he gets too far ahead of us,' Garson mused. 'My personal view is that your ruse might come off, Hargraves, and here's why: Cole is a murderer already. For that reason he won't care how many he wipes out so long as he destroys the evidence before Judith can start talking. To reach the hospital from this laboratory will not present any problems. Yes. I think it's worth a gamble. In fact, it's the only gamble we can take if we're to get Cole in the very act of using this place.'

'Right!' Hargraves decided. 'Then let's get out of here. Harry, get someone to get the front door fixed — we have to leave no clue that we've been.' He smiled faintly as Garson gave an approving nod, and concluded:

'First I'll tell Mrs. Mackinley what we're going to do and get her co-operation: then I'll have a word with the hospital house doctor. After that we'll shovel the whole thing to the press and watch what happens.'

16

By about midnight Hargraves had got everything sorted out to his satisfaction. Mrs. Mackinley had been briefed, and so had the house doctor at the hospital — who, incidentally, had no further news to give with regard to Judith.

She was still in the grip of deep amnesia. Finally, Hargraves had given his carefully calculated statement to the press, and there now remained nothing except to wait — and if possible get a decent night's sleep.

This last endeavour proved a forlorn hope as far as Hargraves was concerned. He had too much on his mind to sleep properly. But he was down at the office as usual the following morning at 9 o'clock, to find Sergeant Brice already there.

'Anything fresh?' Hargraves tossed his hat on to the peg.

'The house doctor rang a few moments ago, sir. He says that he has followed your instructions exactly and that there is no change to report in Miss Mackinley's condition.'

'Hmmm . . . ' Hargraves sat down and tugged two leading morning papers from his pocket. 'Seen the papers, Harry?'

'Some of them, sir. I suppose all of them carry the story?'

'All the important ones, anyway. I've no fear but what Cole will read one of them. We can't expect much action until this evening, anyway, since Judith isn't supposed to make her confession until 9 o'clock tonight.'

'I rather wondered about that, sir. Isn't Cole going to think that a queer time for Judith to start talking?'

Hargraves grinned. 'Evidently you haven't read the reports very closely. That time has been chosen because the doctors are, supposedly, going to spend all today getting her in fit shape to talk. And then again, she is not going to speak until after her father's funeral, which is at 3 o'clock this afternoon. I think it's all quite logical, Harry. Logical enough, anyway, to convince a very anxious man like Cole.'

★　★　★

At last it came to evening. Hargraves still waited for news from his men watching the laboratory-bungalow — and the news came at 8.30. Cole had arrived at the required rendezvous and his car had mysteriously disappeared.

'Right!' Hargraves said promptly, slamming down the telephone. 'This is it, Harry! He's swallowed the bait!'

In a matter of moments they were in their car, moving at top speed to Garson's home. He also was instantly ready, and in 20 minutes flat Brice was swinging the car into Embankment Road, and jammed on the brakes. Immediately a man who had been in concealment came hurrying forward under the street lights.

'Anything?' Hargraves asked briefly, alighting to the pavement.

'Nothing to report, sir. Cole went in and he hasn't come out. Hope you're not too late?'

'Unlikely to be that,' Garson said. 'Take him a long time to get his apparatus centered and the power on. We'll be in time. Let's go, Hargraves.'

As they moved toward the dark, apparently deserted bungalow, Garson said: 'Incidentally, I'm carrying a gun with me. I'm doing it for the safety of the lot of us. Restrictions don't apply in a situation like this.'

Hargraves did not say anything. They stopped within a foot of the bungalow, and scrambled quickly out of the car.

As they moved close to the window they noted how completely the one-way glass blocked any chance of seeing what was going on beyond.

'I'll take the lead for the moment,' Garson said, and with that he ducked down and found the electric wire. As he had done the previous night, it only took him a moment to create a short-circuit, then he straightened and smashed his gun against the window glass. Immediately a flood of light came forth, and beyond stood Cole, in startled wonder, busy at his switch panel.

'Don't move,' Garson snapped, his gun steady; then he motioned Hargraves and Brice forward.

They smashed out the remainder of the window glass and then clambered through, with Garson following behind them.

'Good evening, gentlemen,' Cole said calmly, complete master of his emotions.

'Shut that thing off!' Hargraves snapped, nodding to the projector.

Cole shrugged and did so. The whine of generators descended down the scale and ceased.

'It doesn't matter anyway,' he said. ' 'I've done all I wanted to do.'

'Have you?' Garson asked cynically. 'I don't think so, Mr. Cole. I have an offsetting interference beam at work, which will not let your apparatus operate. Presumably you have aimed your beam at Miss Mackinley, regardless of anybody in the way. It will interest you to know that you can't have done any damage.'

Cole's expression slowly changed. It was plain he had never even contemplated the possibility of being defeated.

'You're under arrest, Cole,' Hargraves said curtly. 'We'll leave right now if you don't mind.'

Cole sighed and glanced around him with regret.

'I suppose I ought to have known I couldn't get away with it. And I had such plans, too. Oh, inspector, would you grant me one favour?'

'What is it?'

'Now you've broken the window there, everything is on view for any prowler to see — and this laboratory contains a good deal of valuable equipment, to say nothing of secrets. Might I be allowed to return the lab to its usual position and leave only an apparently empty bungalow?'

'He'd better do it,' Garson said, as Hargraves demurred. 'We need this lab intact to make good use of these scientific secrets later.'

Cole gave a coldly cynical smile and waited. Then at length Hargraves gave a nod. 'All right — get busy.'

Cole turned to the hydraulic apparatus — and at the same moment it seemed to the three men by the window as though the earth opened beneath them.

In fact it did — or at least the floor did.

They went plunging down into a wide trap, down into darkness as the trap sprang shut behind them.

Dazed by the fall, and in pitch darkness, they floundered to their feet, listening to a creaking, grinding noise and — overhead — a quick rush of footsteps and then silence.

'Where are we?' demanded the voice of Brice. 'What's happened?' —

'Floor trap,' Hargraves answered him briefly. 'Obviously Cole was prepared for the contingency of being caught and part of the floor by the window must have been hinged. While fiddling with the hydraulic system he had merely to release a switch — and here we are!'

'Cole's got away,' Garson added, 'but we're not going to unless we do something quickly.'

He was silent for a moment, and it was a silence that enabled them all to hear the rumble of mechanism and the squeaking, squeegee note of a hydraulic system in action.

Hargraves felt his nerves tighten. Quickly he reached upwards and with his fingertips he could now touch the underside of the slowly lowering laboratory floor. In a matter of seconds he could touch it with the flat of his hands as it creaked lower — and still lower.

'I've a gun that might do something to blast a way,' Garson went on. 'If only we had a light.'

He searched frantically with his fingers and at length came into contact with the thin line that meant a division in the flooring. Even as he made the discovery he, Hargraves and Brice were forced to flatten out, face upwards, so low had the floor sunk.

'I'll risk it!' Garson panted, and his gun exploded with violent force in the confined space. Once, twice, three times — A jagged rent of gray appeared against the total black.

'Shove!' Garson gasped. 'Shove — kick!'

With desperate, last-minute energy all three of them put every ounce of their strength into smashing away the remainder of the trap floorboarding. It was difficult because so little room was left in which to manoeuvre — but with death as the solution if they failed, they accomplished miracles.

Savagely they kicked out the boarding which Garson's revolver had already half shattered.

They tore at the woodwork with their hands, ripping their nails and gashing their flesh, until they had just sufficient room to permit egress of one man.

'Quick, Hargraves!' Garson panted, and without waiting for argument he shoved the inspector's head and shoulders through the gap.

Hargraves moved as fast as he possibly could; and Brice followed after him. The flooring had nearly descended to the limit as Garson clawed his way into the opening, and possibly he would never have made it had not Hargraves and Brice seized him and pulled with all their strength.

With only inches to spare, his left foot came free as the laboratory reached the limit and touched the concrete below.

Garson moved across to the hydraulic apparatus and studied it for a moment.

Then with a nod to himself, signifying that he understood the operation, he pressed a button. Instantly the floor began to rise again and in a moment or two, was at ground level.

'Okay — through the window,' he said, and they wasted no time in scrambling through it. Barely had they done so when a lurching figure came toward them in the street lights: In another moment he was revealed as the man to whom they had spoken earlier.

'You — you gentlemen okay?' he asked, with an effort.

'Still living,' Hargraves assented. 'But where's Cole? Didn't you see him dash out of here?'

'Yes, sir. I tried to stop him but he knocked me out! He must have taken your patrol car.'

'Hell and damnation! I didn't think to lock it when we came here to arrest Cole,' Hargraves said, and scowled with self-recrimination.

His scowl lifted as the officer added: 'As soon as I recovered I dashed back to my car and telephoned the Yard, sir, and tipped them off as to what had happened.'

'Good man! Then he'll not get far,' Hargraves said. 'Scotland Yard will have alerted the whole patrol system as to the registration number of my personal car. Wherever Cole tries to dodge, if he uses the patrol car all the time, we've got him hemmed in . . . '

He paused as the officer winced slightly and fingered the back of his head.

'Are you sure you're all right, son?'

The officer smiled ruefully. 'I've a lump the size of an egg where he struck me, but I'll be okay, sir. My car's over there where I parked it for the surveillance operation — ' he nodded his head in its direction — 'If I can give you a lift anywhere?'

Hargraves looked down at his lacerated hands. 'My fingers are killing me, so the hospital might not be a bad idea. Come on, Harry — let's get out of here.'

They started moving but Garson did not follow them. Instead he turned back toward the bungalow.

'I'll take a look at Cole's car,' he said. 'I want to check on that generator for evidence. And I'll also restore the bungalow to normal in case of prowlers.'

17

'Within half an hour, or less, Cole ought to be nailed,' Hargraves said, as he and Brice waited outside the bungalow for the patrolman to return with his car.

He paused and looked round as a supercharged racer suddenly came into view, its engine snorting, and Garson at the wheel. He skidded to a stop as he saw Brice and Hargraves.

'Thought I might as well dig Cole's car out,' he said with a grin. 'Exchange is no robbery — By the way, it has got an auxiliary generator just as I thought, quite powerful enough for the purpose I suggested. Okay, where do we go?' he questioned.

Hargraves hesitated as the patrolman's car drew up alongside.

'Maybe we should go with Garson, sir,' Brice said. 'His car looks faster — '

Hargraves reflected swiftly, and nodded. 'Better take us to the hospital, Garson.

Two reasons. One, to get our hands professionally fixed and, two, to make sure that Judith Mackinley didn't suffer any harm.' He turned to the patrolman in the other car. 'Follow us there — you need medical attention yourself.'

As Hargraves jumped into the front seat beside Garson — Brice getting into the rear of the car — the scientist gave him a sideways glance.

'The girl couldn't have come to any harm,' he protested. 'Not with my interference in action.'

'I'd like to be sure just the same.'

The scientist shrugged, looked at his grazed and blood-smeared hands, then let in the clutch. With a roar of power the racer shot into the next street; then almost immediately Hargraves and Brice peered intently ahead at a receding pair of rear lights.

'That's our patrol car!' Brice exclaimed in amazement. 'How come Cole's still in the area?'

'He must have been spotted when he tried to get away earlier,' Hargraves said tensely. 'He's doubled back — '

Garson gave a tight grin. 'He won't get away from us in this car,' and pressed his foot hard to the floor. The powerful engine roared and the racer leapt forward in hot pursuit.

The traffic lights ahead changed to red: Cole ignored them and went straight on. So did Garson, screaming the racer from under the nose of a bus radiator ... There lay ahead now a three-mile stretch of four-lane road straight into the heart of the city, and Cole's only chance lay in reaching the city first and losing himself in the dense traffic. Once there high speed would be impossible.

'No you don't!' Garson murmured, his jaw set — and he sent the racer flying down the vista at 105 miles an hour. The distance from the patrol car narrowed by leaps and bounds for there was no possible way in which Cole could get any more speed out of the squad car.

'We've as good as got him!' Hargraves breathed tensely, above the roar of wind and tires. 'He'll never — What's he doing?' He broke off, startled.

He had good reason to ask. Abruptly the squad car was lurching wildly from side to side, swinging far out into the crown of the road.

'Tire's gone!' Brice shouted. 'Look!'

Even as the three men in the hurtling racer watched ahead of them, fascinated, the squad car slewed around to the wrong side of the road, nor did it pull out of the violent skid.

With terrific impact it crashed against one of the tall lighting pylons, bringing it down in a shower of sparks. Instantly the squad car stopped, amid flames and flying metal.

Garson, sweat wet on his face, put on the brakes and screeched to a standstill a dozen yards from the collision. He jumped out and began to run forward; then stopped and retreated from the seething blaze.

'I'm afraid that's it for Cole,' he said, as Hargraves and Brice came hurrying over to join him.

★ ★ ★

We do hope that you have enjoyed reading this large print book.

Did you know that all of our titles are available for purchase?

We publish a wide range of high quality large print books including:

Romances, Mysteries, Classics
General Fiction
Non Fiction and Westerns

Special interest titles available in large print are:

The Little Oxford Dictionary
Music Book, Song Book
Hymn Book, Service Book

Also available from us courtesy of Oxford University Press:

Young Readers' Dictionary
(large print edition)
Young Readers' Thesaurus
(large print edition)

For further information or a free brochure, please contact us at:

Ulverscroft Large Print Books Ltd.,
The Green, Bradgate Road, Anstey,
Leicester, LE7 7FU, England.
Tel: (00 44) 0116 236 4325
Fax: (00 44) 0116 234 0205

reminders, too, in the world of science, as his discoveries are fully examined. There can be no doubt that Jefferson Cole was a genius, but he went the wrong way about using it. As for you, I don't doubt upon your full recovery that you'll find there are plenty more fish in the sea.'

THE END

just enough shock to restore her memory. So in that, at least, it has proved useful.'

'Both my mother and Dr. Taylor here have been telling me what has been going on,' Judith said. 'How far have you got? Have you arrested Jeff?'

'Prepare yourself for a shock,' Hargraves said quietly. 'Cole met his death tonight in trying to elude arrest.' He paused as Judith gave a little gasp and put a hand to her face.

'You'll read all about it in the papers tomorrow,' he said gently. 'We know where the gold is, and it will shortly be restored. We have reason to think we'll restore Grantham's gold, too.'

Judith did not seem to be listening.

'Jeff dead,' she muttered. 'I can't believe it. In spite of all he did to me . . .'

'Don't let your heart rule your head, Miss Mackinley,' Garson said briefly. He came forward and perched on the foot of her bed.

'For the rest of your life you'll carry a memory of Jefferson Cole, in that you'll do everything left-handed instead of right. You will have frequent other

Nearly an hour later Hargraves, Brice and Garson were shown into the private room where Judith Mackinley lay.

The three men were looking subdued, somewhat dirty, and their hands were neatly bandaged.

'Hello, Chief Inspector,' she said, as he pondered her.

He gave a start. 'Then — then you remember me?'

She nodded slowly. 'Quite suddenly this evening I remembered everything. The amnesia completely lifted.'

'Which is something I don't understand,' the house doctor confessed. 'Glad though I am that it has happened.'

Garson asked: 'At what time did the amnesia lift?'

'It would be about 8.30.'

'Does it signify?' Hargraves asked, and the scientist nodded.

'Definitely so. It means my interference beam is not quite so efficient as I thought it was. That was approximately the time Cole switched on his apparatus. And this is the result! Instead of killing Miss Mackinley, as was intended, it produced